FROM
CONSTANTINE'S
CASEBOOK

The Great Sheep Panic

FROM
CONSTANTINE'S
CASEBOOK

The Great Sheep Panic

NATALIE BRIANNE

Searose Press

MMXXI

Author's Note

Dear Reader,

Before you begin, I want to make sure that you are aware of some spoilers.

This story takes place between Flashes of Memory (Book 2) and There Comes a Midnight Hour (Book 3). As such, it contains some significant spoilers for those who haven't finished the first two books in the Constantine Capers series.

If you're new to the series or haven't completed Book 2 yet, I recommend reading that first so you don't find out "who-dun-it" on accident.

For those of you who are caught up—welcome back! This is one of my favorite things I've ever written and still makes me chuckle manically when I read it. I hope you enjoy reading it as much as I enjoyed writing it.

Happy reading!

Natalie Brianne

P. S. No really, this novella spoils the first two books in the Constantine Capers series. Read those first!

November 7, 1888

"You're letting me win," Mira said, leaning over to place her piece on the board.

Byron laughed and leaned back, studying her. "What makes you say that?"

"Your last three moves weren't thought through. If you'd been paying attention, I never would have crowned that last piece. So, either you're distracted, or you're doing this on purpose." She shifted on the sofa, hair falling into her face. He suppressed the urge to reach across the table and tuck the loose curls behind her ear. Instead he forced his attention back to the game board. She was right: he was losing, and badly.

Just over a week before, he woke up wondering what he was missing, and remembered, *actually remembered,* what that something was. *Who* that someone was. He remembered *her.* Mira.

It flooded back to him in waves. Every memory, precious moment, and argument. Each brush of their hands. And yes, since that brilliant October morning his memory hadn't been perfect. Some days he recalled everything down to the exact detail. Others, he needed to be nudged in the right direction in order to find his way to the correct memory. But in any case, Mira stayed at the forefront of his mind, and he prayed that he would never forget her again.

So perhaps that was the reason he was so distracted. Now that he had a memory, he wanted to remember her in this moment.

He wanted to remember the way the afternoon sun slipped through the window and fell onto her skin, making her hair shine and her eyes sparkle. His mind made a careful catalogue of the twist of her mouth and the way her nose scrunched up as she decided on her next move. And the subtle rouge that crept up her cheeks as she caught him staring. Again.

She cleared her throat. "It's your move, Byron."

"Oh." He dragged his gaze down again. Draughts. They were playing draughts. "Right."

He placed a finger on top of one of his pieces, contemplating his next move. He hopped two of her pieces, set them to the side, and glanced up at her.

She had leaned back against the sofa that she called prison, her injured foot up on an ottoman in front of her. He could just make out the bandages above her shoe. Her gaze was set on the window.

"How will we ever catch him?" she whispered.

The "him" in question was most certainly Alexander Durant. Byron had to consciously stop his jaw from tightening. Durant was a liar, murderer, and manipulator who had used Mira to his own twisted advantage. Byron couldn't help but wonder what would have happened if Durant's true colours hadn't surfaced when they did. Would Mira have chosen Alexander over him? A hollow feeling settled in his stomach at the thought.

That line of questioning aside, Durant had fled to France, apparently under Circe's orders. Unfortunately, they hadn't been able to follow. Scotland Yard was still negotiating with the French police, and while Byron could go on his own, he hated leaving Mira with her still healing ankle. Under Landon, the butler's, careful orders, she was to remain on bedrest for at least another two weeks. Perhaps even three, which meant that it would be quite impossible to travel to France until she could walk on her own. And that wasn't even taking into account her Uncle Cyrus and whether he could be convinced to allow her to make the trip at all.

Byron didn't want to leave her. Not now.

"It is a difficult prospect to be certain, but I doubt that it's impossible. We'll find him."

"But how, Byron?" She slammed down her next move, making the table rattle. "At this point he could be halfway to Australia."

And good riddance, he thought, tilting his head to the side. "If Circe ordered him to go to France, he'll stay there until ordered otherwise. We just need to track down Circe's whereabouts in Paris and corner him." He glanced at the board. "Just like how you've managed to pin me in. Goodness, Mira. I think that's the game."

She hummed. "Yes, you do seem to be blocked there, don't you?"

The door behind him opened, and Byron turned to look at the newcomer.

"Oh good! I was hoping you two would still be in here." Walker came in, pressed a kiss to his sister's forehead, and seated himself in an armchair.

"As if Landon would let me go anywhere else," Mira huffed, arms folded as she glowered at her bandaged foot. "If it were spring, maybe he'd let me on the veranda." She sighed. "I wish it were spring."

"Maybe this will cheer you up." Walker ignored his sister's complaints and held up a packet of papers.

Mira's eyes lit up as she reached for it. "Is that the new edition?"

Walker nodded with a grin but made no move to hand it to her.

"What is it?" Byron asked.

"The Magazine of Art," Mira said. "I've been waiting for it for ages! Give it here, Walker."

"I'll hand it over, but first I need your help." Walker held the magazine over her head.

"What sort of help?" Mira's eyes glinted with suspicion.

"I'd say it has something to do with Miss Renaldi." Byron continued to tidy up the game board.

Walker furrowed his brow, hands dropping. "I'm not that easy to read, am I?"

"No, just predictable." Mira snatched the magazine out of his hands.

Byron's eyes flicked over Walker's attire. "You've got a dusting of white powder on your upper sleeve. Looks like it may have rubbed off if she leaned against you while you were on a walk. It was a guess, nothing more."

Walker grinned. "Well, you're right in any case." He turned towards Mira. "I was wondering if you could help me with this." He pulled a small book decorated with floral motifs from his inside pocket.

Mira's shoulders slumped. "Is that all?"

"Her parents have the silly notion that we need a chaperone. And not just any chaperone. No, they had to go and choose her Aunt Eleanor! She's simply dreadful, Mouse. Can't even be within three feet of Liza without getting the evil eye! We barely managed to escape her this morning. So, we need to come up with a different way of communicating."

"Flowers?" Mira groaned and ran a hand over her face.

"You were the one who introduced me to the concept of flower language."

"Only after Byron brought it to my attention." She focused on the magazine, flipping through the pages. Byron caught sight of several black and white art plates as she skimmed.

Walker whirled on him, one eyebrow raised in incredulity. Byron shrugged as he stood and slipped the draughts box back onto the shelf.

"My mind has a strange sense of taste when it comes to what I remember."

"Right." Walker shook his head and turned back to his sister, opening the book. "I think I know what I want to say, but I'm not entirely certain what flowers are in season. I figured you would know."

"And what would make you think that?"

". . . you're a girl?"

Mira looked up from her magazine, unimpressed. "Why don't you simply go to a flower shop and see what's available? Then you can look up their meanings and figure out what to choose from there."

Walker blinked and sat back in the armchair. "I'm an idiot."

"Only just." Mira smirked.

"You may want to ensure that both of you have the same dictionary." Byron leaned against the mantle. "If you don't, you may be unable to communicate."

"I hadn't thought of that!" Walker's eyes widened. "I suppose I ought to go buy us matching copies."

"Or you could simply buy her favorite flower. Why over complicate it?" Mira asked.

"Two reasons. One: You know Liza. She lives for these kinds of secret communications. The complication is half the fun for her. Two: Her favorite flower is even harder to get a hold of than yours."

"What's her favorite?" Mira tilted her head to the side, looking rather like a curious bird.

"Orchids."

Mira hummed. "Yes, that would be difficult. And expensive."

Byron fiddled with his cuffs in an attempt to seem nonchalant. "What are your favorite flowers, Mira?"

"Camellias. And they aren't all that hard to get. It's just that my favorite type only blooms in late fall."

"So around now?" Byron wracked his brain for the nearest flower shop. Perhaps bringing some life into the sitting room would help tide Mira over until she could recover.

"Oh, probably in a week or so. And then a few days for them to be available in flower shops." She slumped into the sofa.

"I guess I'm off to a flower shop then." Walker stood and dusted off his trousers. "Are you staying for dinner, old chap?"

Byron shook his head. "I believe I've leaned on your hospitality enough in the past week."

"Nonsense." Walker clapped him on the back, then leaned in to stage-whisper. "You're keeping my sister sane in her incarceration."

Walker narrowly dodged a well thrown pillow as he exited the sitting room. Byron laughed and retrieved the discarded cushion, placing it on an armchair as he sat across from Mira again. She bit back her own laugh, he supposed, in an attempt to appear more bothered than she was. She marked her spot in the magazine and set it on the table.

"In all seriousness, you are always welcome here, Byron. Especially right now."

"Oh, I'm perfectly aware of that. And I'd be content to stay here with you forever. However, I believe I have some things back at Palace Court that need my attention."

"Ah yes. Any new cases?" She fidgeted with her hands, a sure sign that she was upset and hiding it. At least from what he remembered.

"It's only a matter of time."

"Mm." She wrapped a handkerchief around her fingers one way, then the other.

"But of course, once I have a case . . ." he trailed off.

She shook her head. "Oh, I know. You won't be able to visit as often."

"Actually, I was going to say that I'll have to come round to consult you about it."

Her head shot up, loose curls bouncing around her chin. "Really?"

"Until you can come to the cases, I believe that I have no choice but to bring the cases to you."

A blush tinged her features from her nose to her ears. Byron smiled at it and consciously created a memory to keep.

Byron's heels clicked along the pavement in beat with his breath. Swan Walk was a bit of a jaunt from Palace Court, and the November chill numbed his cheeks. But he grinned in spite of himself. He was well and truly gone, taken, smitten, and every other word that crossed the romantic poets' lips. What a wonderful, glorious thing!

He took the steps up to Palace Court two at a time and plucked the mail from the letterbox before escaping to the warm interior of the front hall. He sifted through the letters before coming to one addressed from Chief Inspector Thatcher.

"Well, Mira, we might have that case sooner rather than later," he muttered, moving to the front room and retrieving the letter opener.

He slipped it under the wax seal and read over the contents.

Constantine,

Things are changing here at the Yard. Come to my office tomorrow at your earliest convenience.

Give my regards to Miss Blayse.

Thatcher

Things were changing, eh? Byron tapped the envelope against his cheek and read over the message again. How?

November 8, 1888

THE SUNLIGHT TRICKLED ONTO HIS DESK AS Byron wrote in his journal. Each evening he wrote down important details and events in one journal, and the next morning he'd write what he remembered on his own in another. He hoped that over time it would continue to improve his memory. The pen scritched over the toothed paper, a glob of ink coming out all over the page.

He hissed under his breath and blotted the ink out. He salvaged what he could of that sentence before setting it aside and pulling out his evening journal to compare notes.

Once again, he remembered Mira without incident. In fact, for the past three days, she had been the first thing on his mind. He smiled to himself and skimmed over the section he had written about her. Then he continued to check his memory.

According to what he had written, he had forgotten two things:

1. *Mira's favorite flowers were Camellias.*
2. *He needed to speak with Thatcher at Scotland Yard.*

All things considered, he hadn't forgotten much from the days previous, but it still vexed him that he had forgotten anything whatsoever. He closed up his notebooks and readied himself and his satchel for the day.

Thatcher was right. Scotland Yard *was* different. Byron couldn't put a finger on it, but there was an uneasy tension in the air.

He didn't like it.

He went straight to Chief Inspector Thatcher's office, greeting Juliet Chickering on the way in.

"Good morning, Mr. Constantine." She smiled up at him.

He glanced at the bouquet of flowers on her desk. Seemed like her relationship was still blooming, thank goodness. He wasn't sure he could handle Juliet-style flirtation every day now that he had some short-term memory. "Good morning, Ms. Chickering. Thatcher in?"

"He's expecting you actually. You can just walk in."

Byron tipped his hat to her and rapped on the door before entering. Thatcher glanced up at him from his paperwork.

"Ah, Constantine. I was wondering when you'd come. Take a seat."

Byron closed the door behind him. "Any news on the Durant front?"

"I'm afraid not. Things have had to be put on pause for the time being."

"Does this have anything to do with your cryptic message?"

"Yes, well." Thatcher cleared his throat. "There have been some rumors going around the yard that Chief Commissioner Warren is going to resign."

Byron hadn't worked much with Commissioner Warren, other than a quick interview when Warren had taken the position in 1886. He had wanted to ensure that Byron really was capable of solving cases without his short-term memory. Granted, Byron only knew about that because he'd read the corresponding journal entry.

"Resign? Why?"

"Politics with the Home Office over the Ripper murders among other things." Thatcher sighed. "I'm just hoping that—" A harsh knock on the door interrupted him.

Juliet poked her head in. "Um. Inspector Thatcher, the Commissioner has asked for everyone to meet in the lobby." She bit her lip.

Thatcher shared a look with Byron. "We'll be down in a moment."

Juliet nodded and closed the door.

Byron let out a long breath. "I guess they aren't just rumors."

The lobby was packed by the time Byron and Inspector Thatcher reached the bottom of the stairs. Byron caught Frederick Wensley's eye and moved through the crowd to stand next to him.

"Hello, Constantine!" Fred clapped him on the back. "Back to the casework already, are we?"

Byron smiled and shook his head. "Thatcher wanted to see me. Said things were changing in the Yard." He gestured to the room. "Seems he was right."

"I'd heard that ol' Warren was resigning, but I didn't believe it. Not until now, that is." Fred stood on his tiptoes. "Wonder who the next Commish will be."

Byron wondered that as well. After all, the new commissioner could change the policy that allowed him to do contracted work through Scotland Yard. While he did receive outside cases, he'd hate to lose the working relationship he had with Thatcher and Fred—and his access to police records.

"Wouldn't it be great if they got Monro back?" Fred said, eyes bright. "I mean, he and Warren had their tiffs, but he was the best of us."

Byron held his tongue, not remembering who "Monro" was. The name seemed familiar though. A hush fell over the crowd as Chief Commissioner Warren stepped up onto a desk at the front. He stood there a moment, surveying the scene, moustache twitching. He was a bit young to be resigning, Byron noted. Although his hair did have a few grey streaks surfacing. Was that recent?

"I'm sure you've already guessed what this meeting is about. Nothing stays secret in the Yard for long." He paused as a wave of chuckles pushed through his audience.

"Yes, I'm resigning. I'll let you all speculate as to why, but that's the long and the short of it. And no," he gave the crowd half a glare, leaning out, "it had nothing to do with the bloodhounds."

The room exploded in laughter, and Warren relaxed, looking over them.

"You lot are some of the best men in the entire country, and I've been proud to serve you and watch this precinct grow. I'll still be around for the next couple of weeks during the transition, so feel free to stop me in the hall. That being said, we have Henry Matthews from the Home Office here to explain what happens next." He nodded once more to the group and stepped off of the desk.

A new man took his place. Older. With an imposing jawline devoid of facial hair. He cleared his throat to settle the crowd. "Well. Thank you for your service, Commissioner Warren. We are still looking into potential candidates for the new commissioner, but expect to have one chosen by the end of the month.

In the meantime, we have chosen an interim commissioner."
He gestured to the side, but Byron couldn't see the individual
through the mass of heads.

"Cassius Parry has worked in the Home Office for the past
twenty-three years. We've tasked him with keeping the peace
here until the new commissioner is appointed." Silence settled
over the room. Matthews coughed. "Dismissed."

With that word, the company disbanded in a noisy
fashion. Fred let out a sigh and trekked back towards the
records room.

"I doubt this Parry fellow has even been to the Yard before
today," Fred said, holding the door open for Byron to follow.

"Ah, but it's only for a few weeks. You ought to be more
worried about the new commissioner, rather than the interim."

"You're right. There's not much—"

Fred was interrupted by Ex-Commissioner Warren entering
the records room, followed by a stout mousy-haired gentleman.

"And this is the records room. We have files going back
thirty years here."

"Hm." The man looked around the room. He nodded at
Fred. "Good afternoon, Constable . . .?"

"Wensley, sir. Frederick Wensley."

"I'm Interim Commissioner Parry. Are you often assigned
to the records room?"

"Once a week or so, sir."

Parry nodded and turned his gaze on Byron. His brow furrowed, and he turned back to Warren. "I thought I had already
met all the inspectors."

Warren rubbed the back of his neck. "You have. Mr. Constantine here is a contracted private detective."

"And what is he doing in the records room?"

Byron cleared his throat, not appreciating being referred to
in the third person. "Constable Wensley and I were merely finishing a discussion, sir."

Parry narrowed his eyes. "Detective Constantine? You're the one with the memory issue, yes?"

Byron's stomach churned and he swallowed. "I have had issues with my short-term memory in the past, sir, howev—"

"I'd like to talk to you. In my office." He turned on his heel and left the room.

Warren stood stock still for a moment, then turned to Byron. "I'm sorry about that. He's a bit abrupt."

"I noticed. Do you know what he wants to talk with me about, sir?"

Warren's eyes softened. "He likely wants to interview you. I wouldn't worry about it too much. The Home Office is well aware of your condition. And your case rate."

Byron let out a breath. Warren turned towards the door.

"I ought to catch up with him. I haven't actually shown him where the office is yet, and he's already gotten lost twice." Warren winked at the two of them and left the room.

Fred let out a laugh. "Well this ought to be interesting."

Interesting was one way to put it. *Memory issue* was what Parry had called it. And the tone in which he said it bothered Byron. He couldn't quite place a finger on why. And what was worse, that short interaction had stripped Byron to his core, revealing a mound of insecurities that he would rather not address. Because even though Byron *knew* he was competent and had a case rate to back up that competency, deep down he still had moments of doubt. What would happen if the interim commissioner found him incapable of working with the Yard?

Fred waved a hand in front of his face. "You alright there, chap?"

Byron forced a smile. "Of course. I just get the feeling that this interview won't be as favorable as the last one."

"Perhaps a bit stiffer, yes. But you heard what Warren said. The Home Office knows what you're capable of."

"Yes, but does Cassius Parry?"

Byron waited outside the commissioner's office. The secretary there, a Miss Lorelei Tawnsing, had told him it would only be a minute. Close to fifteen minutes later, the door opened, and Cassius Parry beckoned him in.

A row of boxes filled with knickknacks and books stood against the wall closest to the door, likely Commissioner Warren's. The desk was bereft of any kind of personal affects. The shelves behind the desk held books all bound in the same material. All of them were the exact same size. Parry took his seat behind the desk in an overstuffed chair and gestured for Byron to sit across from him.

"So, Detective Constantine," he drawled. "How long have you worked with the Yard?"

"On and off since 1882, sir." Byron maintained eye contact, sitting up straight.

"On and off? And what precluded your ability to work consistently?"

Byron resisted the urge to pinch the bridge of his nose. He knew very well that Parry was aware of exactly what stopped him from working with the Yard consistently.

"Well sir, there was an incident in 1884 that caused some issues with memory retention. Directly after the accident, I took a few months off in order to attend to that. Doctor's visits, personal issues, and the like."

"I see. Is this why you are not a permanent detective in the Yard?"

"I prefer to work on my own in any case, but yes."

The interim commissioner hummed. "And would you describe your 'memory issues' to me?"

"Until recently, I could only retain present memories if I did not sleep. As you might expect, that made it rather difficult to remember the day-to-day details. I remedied this by using a journal and hired a secretary to help me keep things straight."

Byron expected him to take notes, but Parry simply stared him down, unflinching.

"And your most recent case," Parry said. "I've been told you suspect a man named Alexander Durant. But that he has seemingly disappeared?"

"He's left for France. I believe Commissioner Warren should have left the necessary documentation. Last I heard the Yard was working on getting in contact with the French police so we could put up a perimeter."

"Yes. But we also have investigated Durant and it seems that he doesn't exist."

"I beg your pardon." Byron leaned forward. "He most certainly does."

"We've sent officers to investigate where you say he worked and to find any records, but I'm afraid that, according to every source, barring you, Alexander Durant never existed in the first place. Not a record of his birth, work history, or living accommodations. And if that's the case, there is no point in contacting the French police, now is there?"

"Excuse me, Commissioner, but is that not proof of Circe's involvement? If they were truly able to erase a man's existence—"

"That's the other thing. This Circe business. It's a little far-fetched, isn't it? The only person who has ever found any evidence of it is you. And with your memory being the way it is . . ."

Byron's shoulders tensed as he fought to keep his temper. "If you're going to insult me, I'd prefer if you just say what you mean instead of talking in circles. Are you saying that I've made the whole thing up?"

"When people have problems with their mental acuity, they generally have more than one issue. I'd imagine that losing one's memory can cause a bit of paranoia. Believing in things that don't exist."

Byron took a deep breath, fists clenched. "If I'm imagining things, then how would you suggest I've solved as many cases as I have?"

"Forgive me, but I find it hard to believe that in your state you've managed to solve any."

"Well, sir, I—"

Parry interrupted. "And I believe we have a good number of qualified inspectors here at the Yard. I'm sorry, Mr. Constantine, but your services are no longer required."

Anger bubbled beneath the surface of Byron's composure. He'd had plenty of people question his abilities in the past but something about Parry seemed different.

"Please excuse me for being impertinent, sir, but I believe you should know something before you force me out without due cause." Byron leaned forward, keeping his voice level. "I have solved over forty cases since my accident, and twenty-six of them were issued to me by the Yard. I can go places where your constables cannot and have resources and informants that you do not have. You can speak with Chief Inspector Thatcher and he'll tell you what I am capable of."

Byron leaned back against the armchair. "Aside from that, my condition has changed. I retain new memories from one day to another without use of external forces. As for this paranoia that you claim I have in regards to Circe or Mr. Durant, I will have you know that I have several eyewitnesses who would vouch for me, including a good number of the men under your *temporary* jurisdiction."

He paused, letting the new information sink in. "If you need to test my abilities, so be it, but do not judge me by your preconceived notions of what you think a detective should look like or be."

Cassius Parry sat in silence for a few moments before standing and moving over to a side table. He shuffled through a stack of casefiles and brought one folder back to the table.

"Very well. I will give you one shot. Flub it and your work with the Yard is over. I have ties with the Home Office that can ensure this policy will stay in place even after the new commissioner is brought in."

He opened the folder. "On November third, thousands of sheep near Reading escaped their paddocks simultaneously in the middle of the night. Vandals couldn't have managed a feat like that." Parry stood and handed the folder to Byron across the desk. "They are calling it the Great Sheep Panic. Solve this, and you'll secure your spot at the Yard."

"And Durant?"

Parry let out a breath and sat back in his chair. "If you manage to prove yourself, I'll personally arrange for a team to be sent to France to search for him and contact the French police. Do we have a deal?"

Byron hesitated only a moment before taking Parry's hand. "We do."

Fred looked between the folder and Byron. "You can't be serious. Sheep?"

Byron shrugged and took the folder back. "I'm afraid so. And if I don't figure this out. Well."

"You won't be able to work with the Yard. But that doesn't mean you can't continue your investigations. There are plenty of other cases out there that you could solve without us."

"That isn't the point. If I don't solve this, I don't have the resources to go after Durant on my own. He'll go free. Especially since Circe has erased any trace of him here in England."

"Oh dear. Did Parry say how long you have?"

"A week. But he did say that I need to take a constable

with me as it is, 'official Yard business.' My guess is he wants someone to spy on my efforts and report back. Hopefully whoever I choose will be friendly." Byron gave Fred a pointed look.

Fred stepped back, turning to sort another shelf of records. "Oh no. No, I'm afraid I'm a bit too busy to be gallivanting over the countryside trying to arrest the big bad wolf."

"I wasn't actually considering you." Byron fiddled with his cuffs. "I was thinking of asking Jenkins."

"Jenkins?! Really?" Fred whirled towards him, disbelief and suspicion flitting over his expression.

Byron nodded, attention straying to readjusting his waist-coat. "In my limited experience with him, he's proven to be competent enough. And he's always been friendly. Aside from that, his family works with sheep so it seems like the best choice."

Fred groaned. "Yes, but you've forgotten how insufferably chatty he is. And his deductive skills are rubbish."

"Do you have a better candidate?" Byron raised an eyebrow.

Fred let out a long-suffering sigh. "Alright, alright. I'll come. When are you leaving?"

"Tomorrow, I think. Best get down there and hunt for clues as soon as possible. The sooner we solve this, the sooner he'll send men after Durant." He smiled. "And besides, who knows what nefarious plot those sheep are up to."

Fred laughed. "I'll meet you at Palace Court tomorrow morning then. Give my regards to Miss Blayse when you go to break the news."

Byron frowned. Right. With this case he'd be leaving London for several days. Hopefully she'd forgive him for investigating a mystery without her.

November 9, 1888

FROM THE MOMENT THE TRAIN SEIZED AND shifted forward, anxiety came over Byron like a disease. A chest tightening, breath stopping, chill-inducing malady. Each turn of the wheels took him away from London, away from the familiar and towards uncertainty. He rubbed his hands over his trouser legs and stared out the window at the scenery moving past.

Why, he'd taken this very line to and from his birthplace in Taunton many times. Once before with Fred, even. But not once since the accident. At least, that he remembered. And yes, now that he had his memory back, he remembered most things. But his miraculous recovery was unprecedented, undocumented, and unreliable. Could this miracle wend its way and disappear entirely, leaving him once more in the dark without his memory?

"If you keep sighing like that, you'll fog up the window, old chap," Fred said, reclining in the opposite seat of the train car. His hat rested just over his eyes, and were it not for the subtle smirk on his lips he may have looked asleep.

Sure enough Byron's breath had condensed on the glass. "Can you blame me for my frustration? I've finally regained some semblance of control over my memory. Why is it *now* that they question my abilities?"

He never had an issue with confidence before regaining his short-term memory. After all, if you can't remember your ineptitude, you are doomed to always believe in your competence. And while it was one thing for *him* to question his own abilities, having the interim commissioner breathing down his neck was ultimately worse. Byron's stomach churned. What if he couldn't solve the case?

"And why sheep?" he added, his annoyance only adding to his melancholic state of mind.

"I rather like sheep, personally. They are terribly clever animals." Fred sat up and rolled the brim of his hat between his fingers. "Why, this 'great sheep panic' as they call it, could very well be the uprising of an ovine criminal empire."

"Be serious, Fred."

"I'm completely serious. As we speak there could be some unscrupulous ewe or homicidal hoggerel roaming the countryside preparing for their next great misdeed." Fred leaned forward, the beginning of a grin visible in the corners of his eyes.

A laugh sprang from Byron's chest as Fred continued. "Now free from their paddocks, there's no telling what they'll do!"

Byron's frame shook with mirth despite his better judgement. "This is utterly ridiculous." He attempted to compose himself.

"No, that would be if we were investigating cows."

Both men erupted in unmanly giggles. The countryside whipped by outside their window. Once their laughter had petered out, Byron sighed again.

"I still wish I could have brought Mira with me."

"Yes, I am a poor substitute for her. How is our dear Miss Blayse, anyhow?"

"Still recovering and going mad staying indoors. But she was entirely supportive of me going to prove my skills to the interim commissioner. When I told her about the subject of our investigation she laughed and said, 'thank goodness it's so mundane, or I might be jealous of you going on such a trip.' Or something to that effect."

Fred grinned. "We'll find a way to make an adventure of it. That way you'll have a story to bring back to her."

Byron nodded and returned his gaze to the window. He'd solved plenty of crimes regardless of his affliction. Still, he'd always had to rely on his journal or Mira. He'd left both back in London, hoping that for once he could solve the case without either crutch. But if something went wrong and he didn't have his journal, what would he do then? He glanced at Fred, the man having turned his attention to a newspaper. Perhaps he didn't need to worry so much. Fred would sort him out if worse came to worse, sheep or not.

Reading was a large market town just southwest of London proper. Between the Great Western Railway and the river barges, it was quickly becoming quite the manufacturing and trading center. And yet, for all the hustle and bustle that reminded Byron of London, there was a calm beauty to it. He looked out to where the Thames met the Kennet and smiled at the way the rivers sparkled in the morning light. Mira would have liked it quite a bit. Probably would have memorized the scene for a later watercolor painting.

With minimal luggage in hand, the two men stood in the town square forming a plan of action.

"I suppose we first need to speak with some of the farmers and investigate the properties in question." Fred turned in a slow circle. "I doubt we'll learn anything in the markets."

"You'd be surprised," Byron said, heading in that direction. Fred followed behind him.

They came up to a row of market stalls with vendors of various goods from bread to flower bulbs. There were quite a few people milling about in spite of the early hour and spitting rain. A few young boys zig zagged between the stalls playing tag. Byron approached an older woman selling knitted goods.

"Excuse me, ma'am, but do you have a minute to answer some questions?"

Her lazy gaze trailed from her knitting up towards his face, wrinkles crinkling as she smiled. "Depends on what those questions are, young man." Her speech was slow and drowsy.

"We heard there was a bit of a panic with the sheep last Saturday and are here to investigate the matter. Do you know anything of it?" Byron asked.

"Oh yes." She set her knitting down and looked up at them with wide eyes. "Never seen anything quite like it before or since. It was an unusual dark night. Most unusual. Sun set 'round four or five, and such a ruckus you've never seen started near eight, I'd say. Such bleating and baaing and rustling. I didn't mind it none, figured they were all spooked by the storm coming in. And if there were a problem, it were Tom's." She paused and picked up her yarn and needles again. "That's me son. He runs the farm nowadays. Next morning, we go out to find fences busted over and the sheep in every which way. I think we still haven't found all of them, poor things."

"About where is your farm located?" Byron asked.

"It's nigh up to Basildon Park. Not part of the estate mind you, but just off it."

"And you can't think of any reason why this would have happened?" Fred asked.

The woman paused. "No, but they are such frightened crea-tures. Could be a wolf or dog or the like." Her brows furrowed. "Course, it happened after those peddlers came through. Shady fellows they were, and Davies just let em stay up in his barn for no good reason."

"Davies?" Byron asked. His fingers itched for a pen to write down the details.

"Harold Davies. He farms the land a few miles south of our farm. Close to Tidmarsh. They begged him for a place to stay, and the fellow just can't say no. They've up and disappeared now. Strangest thing."

Byron and Fred shared a look. Fred cleared his throat. "That is rather odd, Mrs.?"

"Chapman. Alice Chapman."

"Thank you very much, Mrs. Chapman."

"Of course." Her focus flicked behind him and she sat forward. "Hey now, Owen Haslam! Adam Nobbs! I see you there with that rat!"

Byron turned just in time to see two of the boys running off, a woman in another stall shrieking as the rat skittered across the ground.

"Those boys," Mrs. Chapman tutted. "They're always playing tricks."

After asking a few other helpful locals for directions and dropping their luggage off at a lodgings house in Tidmarsh, Fred and Byron ended up on the Davies farm. As they made their way over the fields they climbed over stiles and around bunches of straw, muddying their boots. They came up to the main house soon enough. An ugly looking bush stood near the door, covered in half formed green cabbage-looking things. Byron stepped past the sad plant and knocked on the door. A middle-aged woman answered the door with a confused look on her face.

"Can I help you?"

"We're looking for Harold Davies. We've been told this is his farm," Byron said.

"That it is." The woman looked between the two of them. "What do you need him for?"

"We're investigating the sheep panic, madam." Fred tipped his hat.

The woman smiled. "That again? It were just lightning, weren't it?"

"That's what we're investigating," Byron said.

"Alright then. Harold and our son, Jack, will be in the north pasture now, I'd say. I'll walk out with ye and bring them their lunch. Just a moment."

She disappeared into the house before returning with a small bundle.

"And what were your names?" she asked them as she led the way through the yard and into another pasture.

"Byron Constantine and Fred Wensley." Byron gestured to himself and then Fred. "We've been sent by Scotland Yard to investigate."

She gave them a once over. "Scotland Yard, eh? A funny thing to send a detective for."

As they moved through the pasture a flock of sheep spotted them and came over, following at a distance. They dispersed as the group approached a man mending a fence. A younger man, about fifteen, was holding it steady and bore a striking resemblance to his father.

"Harold! Jack!" the woman called. "I've got your lunches here! And there's two gentlemen to see you."

Both straightened and looked over. "That I see. What can I do for the two of ye?" Mr. Davies said, voice gruff.

"We're here about the sheep, sir," Fred offered.

"The sheep?" Jack furrowed his brow.

"Yes," Byron said. "What can you tell us about what happened on November third?"

Mr. Davies narrowed his eyes and scratched the back of his head. "Why, that were the night that the sheep went off kilter!" He moved closer, wiping the dirt off his hands and taking the lunch bundle from his wife. He unwrapped it, passed Jack his portion, and began to eat while he talked. "It were 'round eight or nine, I'd say. Well after the sun set. Blackest night I've seen in a while, and then we hear a commotion out here. Come morning, the sheep are scattered over hill and dale, stuck in hedgerows—why, there were even one up a tree!"

"It was not up a tree, Harold," Mrs. Davies laughed. "It was a close thing though. With 'em all up in bushes and scattered about, we spent the whole morning tracking them down."

"Aye, that's right," Mr. Davies said with a sigh.

Jack bit into his sandwich, shrinking back from the conversation.

Mr. Davies continued. "Part of me wonders if it were those peddlers."

"Can you tell me about them?" Byron asked.

"What, the sheep?" Davies pointed further up the pasture. "They're over yonder, no worse for wear other than a bit of dirt."

"No," Byron hid a laugh. "The peddlers. Do you often house travelling salesmen?"

"Oh, them. Not usually, no. They come in from another town, bustling up the mud in their covered cart, and I tell 'em I'm not interested in their wares, regardless of what they sell. They didn't push or nothing, didn't even try to sell me anything at all. Just asked if they could stay in the barn. I tell 'em that's where the farm hands stay, when we have them that is, and they say they'd be happy to do some work in exchange for the lodging for a week. I say that there ain't much work this time of year, but maybe they could find some work and better lodgings up at the Chapman farm. After all, it's just Tom that's got that whole acreage since his father, Grant, died last October. I said they might have better luck there."

He sighed and wrapped up what was left of his lunch and handed it off to his wife before returning to his work at the fence. Jack joined him a moment later, still warily eying Byron and Fred.

Mr. Davies continued. "But these two fellows were real persuasive. Said they'd do any work I could find for them in exchange for a week in the barn. So, I think on it a moment, and I tell them if they can help me prep the sheep for the barge, they could stay."

"Barge?" Fred asked.

"Aye, it's about time for slaughtering. We don't do it ourselves. Got an abattoir in Bristol does it for us, and distributes. There's a barge that goes up the Kennet and Avon canal through to there, and we like to get the sheep that are ready there early November. I were meant to be taking them yesterday, but the barge was delayed some by the sheep panic. Won't be leaving until the twelfth now." He scratched his head before continuing. "Strangest thing, those two. Usually, peddlers don't stick to one place for long. And aside from that, they worked for me during the day. No time to sell their wares at all. And then, before the week was out, they up and disappeared right during this sheep nonsense."

"I'd have said they were two troublemakers," Mrs. Davies said. "Playing some kind of practical joke on us honest folk by letting the sheep out in that kind of storm."

Jack lost his grip on the fence post, and Mr. Davies swore as he tried to correct it. "Careful there, lad. Keep it straight."

Byron cocked his head. "You said it was a practical joke, then?"

Mrs. Davies let out a sigh. "I thought it was until I heard

that this same thing happened all round this part of the county. They couldn't very well organize a whole group of ne'er-do-wells in every farm 'round Reading, now, could they?"

"Certainly not," Byron said. "But it is odd how the peddlers insisted on sleeping in your barn. Is there anything nearby you could imagine would be worth something to them? Anything particular about this farm?"

Mr. Davies finished up his work on the post and shrugged. "It's the same as any farm 'tween London, and Bristol, I'd reckon. Nothing more common than sheep round these parts."

"Hmm." Byron turned in place. "Where are the paddocks located?"

"They're close to the barn. We'll be heading that way next to put away this mess if you wanted to come with us."

Byron nodded and moved forward to help carry supplies.

"Oh, thank ye," Mr. Davies said. "But me and Jack can handle it. Barn's just this way." He plodded off towards the barn in the distance, Jack following close behind.

"I'll be in the house if you need anything," Mrs. Davies said before picking up her skirts and moving away.

Byron and Fred fell behind Harold and Jack by a few paces.

"What do you make of it?" Byron whispered.

"I think lightning is as good an explanation as any, but I'm not an expert on sheep," Fred said. "To be quite honest, I think a more interesting mystery lies with the peddlers."

"I agree. Although I think young Jack knows something."

"You'd say?" Fred asked, looking towards the boy.

"There isn't a reason for him to be so nervous, and yet he's twitchy."

They quickened their pace to catch up with the elder and younger Davies, who were putting the tools away.

"The paddocks are just through here." Mr. Davies pushed open the side door and led them around back.

Byron moved over to the gate and examined it. Seemed

sturdy enough. There were definite marks on it and the other fence posts, likely from the sheep's hooves. The bracers between fence posts were spaced well enough that the sheep couldn't get through them without hurting themselves. Despite that, clumps of wool clung to the splintered surface as if the sheep had pushed their way through.

"Must have been quite the scare to have them running like that," he said, scratching his head and looking out over the fields.

"Aye, that it was. But I don't understand it meself." Mr. Davies leaned against the fence. "You see, we get storms of these types all times of year and this has never happened before."

"So we've gathered," Fred said. "Although both you and Mrs. Chapman mentioned it being a darker night than usual. Perhaps the lightning, in stark contrast with the darkness, frightened them more."

"Tis a fair thought," Davies hummed.

Jack came out of the barn, having finished putting away the tools.

Byron gestured up to the wooden structure. "Is this where the peddlers slept?"

"That it is."

"And what were their names?" Byron asked.

"Hugh and Liam Walter. Brothers, I think." He adjusted his suspenders.

"Thank you, Mr. Davies. Do you mind if we take a look around the barn?"

"I don't mind at all, long as you leave everything where it is. If there weren't anything else, we ought to get back to work." Mr. Davies turned to leave and Byron took a step forward.

"Just one other thing. May we borrow Jack for a moment?"

The younger man stiffened at his name.

Mr. Davies cocked his head to the side. "I'll be in the west field." He nodded to his son and left in that direction.

Jack was pale and shaky.

Byron leaned against the paddock. "So, Jack. Are you friends with the boys on the other farms?"

"Aye," Jack said, voice trembling.

"Haslam and Nobbs?"

The boy nodded and took off his cap. "And Langton."

Byron paused a moment. "I hear that you lot like to play pranks. Harmless ones, of course," he amended, trying not to spook him.

Jack wrung his cap in his hands. "It never hurts nobody."

Fred grinned. "Of course not. The two of us got into a fair bit of trouble ourselves." He turned to Byron. "You remember that toad I caught down by the River Tone?"

"I couldn't forget it. After all, I got the blame for it." Byron rolled his eyes.

"Blame? For a toad?" Jack asked, shoulders relaxing.

"Well, it wasn't just the toad," Fred said. "You see, Byron's father was the reverend, and he had Mrs. Dervish up at the parish to discuss the church bazaar over tea. We snuck into the kitchen when the cook wasn't looking and put the poor toad in the teapot."

Jack's eyes widened. "You didn't."

"You should have seen the look on her face when the pot started croaking. It was a masterpiece."

The story worked a charm and soon the three were laughing like co-conspirators.

"So," Byron said, "we've told you about one of our pranks. I think it's time you told us about one of yours. What were you and your friends up to on the third of November?"

Jack shifted from one foot to the other. "Promise not to tell me dad?"

"It can be our secret," Fred said, putting a finger to his lips and winking.

Jack took a deep breath. "A few weeks ago, Haslam heard

his uncle talk about the minds of sheep. Said they are uncommonly clever, but if one flock did something, it can affect another. We was out in Chapman's apple grove, climbing a tree the Saturday before and we got to talking. If we scared one flock, would it spook the next? And what if we did it to all our flocks? What then?" He kicked the dirt. "We didn't know it would go 'cross the whole county. Or that it would stop the barge from leaving on time."

Byron shook his head. "And you're worried about what your father will do if he finds out?"

"That's it exactly, sir! None of our sheep got hurt, but it's been such a mess."

"You're a good lad, Jack," Fred said. "We won't tell."

"Thank ye!" Jack grinned. "I'd best get down to me dad. He'll be waiting for me."

"Off you go," Byron said.

Jack put his cap back on his head and ran off to the west field.

"That's a new record, I'd say," Fred said as the lad ran off. "Less than a day here and the mystery is solved."

"One mystery is solved. But there is another." Byron clapped Fred on the back and led the way into the barn.

"Ah, yes." Fred followed him in. "We still have the issue of the Walter brothers, don't we?"

"Exactly. It seems odd that they were so focused on this farm in particular." Byron stood at the base of the ladder that led to the hayloft. He jostled it to test its rigidity and decided to trust it, climbing to the top.

"Think we'll find anything in here?" Fred asked, poking around on the main level.

"I'm hoping so. After all, we need something to bring back to Parry."

"You're not going to tell him about the boys?"

"From my limited interactions with Parry, I think he'll want to punish those boys harshly. Maybe even give them some time. They didn't do any harm in the end, and I'd hate to break Jack's confidence. We can tell Parry that it was lightning, case closed."

"Somehow, I doubt the interim commish will take that as proof of your ability," Fred said from the opposite side of the barn, where he examined a few empty stalls.

"You may be right about that . . ." Byron trailed off, eyes catching something beneath the hay. "But maybe he'll accept a different mystery."

He stooped to the floor of the loft and brushed the hay aside. A golden frame with incredible workmanship lay beneath, empty save for the bits of hay that poked through from the loft floor.

Fred came up the ladder and whistled. "Rumpelstiltskin has been busy."

Byron lifted the frame and examined the inside. The back-side lacked the gold sheen of the front. Gilded then. Nails lined the inner edge with strings of canvas caught along them. Flecks of paint clung to some of the strings. Byron set the frame down and glanced up at Fred. "Think Parry would be interested in us catching some art thieves?"

Fred's eyes lit up. "Art thieves?" He crouched and picked up the frame himself. "You'd think they would have disposed of the frame better."

Another glint of light caught Byron's eye. "Frames." He grabbed a pitchfork and moved further into the hayloft. Moving the hay around, he uncovered three more frames of varying sizes. "I would say they might have had no choice but to leave them here, but evidently they had enough time to remove the paintings properly."

"How do you mean?"

Byron picked up another frame. "If this was a rushed job, they would have cut the paintings from the frames. Instead, they carefully removed them from the nails around the edge.

Less damage overall, greater profit, but greater risk with the time spent."

"So then why did they leave the frames? The Davies would have found them sooner or later."

"Perhaps they are counting on it being later. Which means we don't have much time to track them down."

Fred dusted off his hands. "Alright. What do we do now?"

Byron moved to sit next to him, legs dangling over the edge of the loft. "I believe Mrs. Chapman mentioned something about an estate in the area. Wasn't it Basildon Park?"

"That sounds right."

"Based on what she said, her farm would be much closer to it than this one."

Fred frowned. "That's odd. You'd think if they were planning on stealing from Basildon they'd choose the farm that was closer."

"I agree. There must be something else at play here. Shall we?"

The trek up to Basildon Park took longer than expected. Byron, for one, was grateful for the exercise and the opportunity to be out in nature. He couldn't remember the last time he'd been to the countryside. His shoulders relaxed, chest unwinding the longer they walked through the autumnal groves. Being surrounded by trees and streams brought great peace to his mind. The dulcet tones of warbling birds sang through the air, and he felt entirely at ease.

Unfortunately, Fred didn't feel the same way. "I bet we could have found a carriage," he said, rubbing his hands together while he caught his breath by a fallen log. "My fingers are freezing."

"It's not that bad. We're almost there at any rate. And aside from that, the colours are beautiful."

Fred glanced up at him. "You've really fallen, haven't you?"

Byron frowned. "What?"

"I know you better than just about anyone, aside from your own mother of course. You've never commented on something just for beauty's sake before."

"Haven't I?"

"Not until you met Miss Blayse." Fred clapped him on the back.

Byron fell silent and followed Fred as he led the way up towards the house, leaves crunching beneath their feet. Fred was right, of course. He had to be. In fact, only a moment before Byron had been contemplating what Mira would think about this walk. What would she say about the way the leaves drifted onto the pond, cascading upon the water and floating on the surface? Would she feel more alive because of the way the sunlight trickled through the branches, sending splotches of light onto the ground below? His gaze flicked up to find a bird singing from its perch on a branch. Had he really never noticed those things before her? Or had he noticed but not found it relevant?

Caught in his thoughts as he was, he didn't realize they'd arrived at the house until his feet hit the gravel path in front of the estate. They paused a moment to catch their breath, and then Fred pulled the bell.

A moment or two passed before the door opened and a stately butler greeted them. He stood straight as a ramrod, with a pressed collar and receding hairline. The white gloves he wore had a faint hint of polish on the fingertips. No stains of any kind stood out on his uniform, but a few scuffs adorned his black leather shoes.

"May I help you?" the butler said.

"Yes. My name is Byron Constantine, and this is Frederick Wensley. We're detectives from Scotland Yard."

The man's eyes widened by a fraction. "I see. I'm afraid that

Miss Morrison is in southern France and will be for the duration of the winter."

"Is that so?" Fred shared a glance with Byron. "Well, I believe that you will probably be able to answer our questions in any case."

The man nodded minutely. "What would you like to know?"

"Before we start, what was your name?" Byron asked.

"You may call me Winterby."

"Well, Mr. Winterby, would you happen to know if a theft has occurred within the past week or so?" Fred asked.

"A theft?" The man furrowed his brow. "If something was stolen, we would have contacted the police immediately."

"Is it possible that you aren't aware of the theft?" Byron asked.

Winterby bristled. "I'm the longest working member of this household, starting as a footman before Mr. Morrison died some thirty years ago. As such, I'm aware of everything that occurs in this house, and in that time, there has never once been a theft."

"Would it hurt anything for us to check?" Fred asked.

"After all," Byron added. "If a theft occurred without your notice, wouldn't you rather know now than when Miss Morrison returns?"

Winterby's shoulders lowered an inch. "There is some wisdom in what you say." His face softened. "Would you care to survey the house with me?"

Byron nodded, and he and Fred followed the old butler into the house, grateful for the protection from the chill November air. After leaving their coats and hats in the hall, they followed Winterby through each of the rooms. He commented on the age of some of the pieces, when and where they were acquired, and the like. It seemed that the late Mr. Morrison had a taste for the arts—Turner and Constable in particular, as well as a few more

Italian inclined painters. They came into a west sitting room and the man paused, mouth gaping.

"There must be a mistake. I would have known before now."

Byron followed his line of sight and found a blank space between two other landscapes. A nail protruded from the wall, and a rectangular area was discolored from the wallpaper around it.

"Do you remember which painting was here?"

"Oh yes," Winterby said. "That was one of Mr. Morrison's most beloved Constable pieces. He bought it for one-hundred and fifty guineas back in 1824."

Byron blinked. "One-hundred and fifty? That's quite a lot."

The old butler nodded. "He bought it on the first day of the exhibition. In fact, it's one of the more famous of the collection. The Magazine of Art highlighted this piece in 1884."

"One of the frames we found in the barn was about that size, wasn't it Byron?" Fred moved over to the wall and measured it with his arms.

Byron frowned. "I'd say it was. But there were four frames in total. Let's keep looking."

Winterby seemed greyer as he led them to the next room. By the time they had surveyed the whole house, they had only discovered two paintings missing. One from that original west sitting room and one on the floor above in a hallway. When they came back to the front room Winterby was shaking, his face a deathly pallor.

"Why don't you take a seat, Mr. Winterby? It is quite a shock."

Winterby obliged, settling his old bones into a nearby armchair, gaze distant.

"Now that I think about it, two of the frames were a different color and style," Fred said. "Perhaps they came from a different estate?"

Byron turned to Winterby, brow furrowing. "What's the nearest estate house to this one?"

Winterby nodded, composing himself. "That would be Englefield House, sir. It's somewhat south of here. If you take Shooter's Hill east to the main road through Tidmarsh, you'll find the estate soon enough."

"We'll have to check with them, but if it is south of Tidmarsh—" Byron glanced at Fred "—that would place the Davies' farm within walking distance of both."

Byron slumped on his bed. It had taken the rest of the day to finish their questioning at Englefield House and return to their lodgings. They had confirmed that two paintings had been stolen without the knowledge of the staff. Four paintings, two peddlers, and no leads as to where they might have gone from there.

Fred shuffled off his shoes across the room, readying himself for bed.

"We'll have to contact the local police in the morning and let them know about the theft." Fred removed his tie and draped it over the bed frame.

Byron nodded. "Perhaps they'll know more about the situation."

"Do you think the thieves have left the area yet?" Fred lay back on his bed, hands behind his head.

Byron twisted his tie in his hands and paced over to the fireplace. "With all the barges and trains, it's possible they've left the country entirely."

"But?" Fred sat up.

"Instinct says they haven't."

"Oh good. I'm not quite ready to go back to London. I think the country air is doing something for me after all."

Byron chuckled and moved to dim the lights.

"Aren't you going to write in your journal?" Fred asked.

Byron stopped with his hand on the switch. "I left it in London. I thought it would be good to try and solve this one without it."

His friend sat up, eyes wide. "Are you sure that's a good idea?"

"I've got to try it at some point. And you'll let me know if I've forgotten anything tomorrow, won't you?"

Fred softened. "Course I will."

Byron flicked the switch. The gas lamps flickered before going dark and Byron settled into bed.

"But I won't promise not to embellish things!" Fred laughed. "Goodnight!"

November 10, 1888

A BIRD TRILLED OUTSIDE THE WINDOW AND BYRON desperately tried to remember where he was and how he got there. This certainly wasn't his bed. He sat up, the early morning light casting eerie shadows through the room. A second bed was on the opposite wall. The form of the person occupying it drifted up and down in a lazy breathing pattern.

The tension in Byron's shoulders relaxed by a fraction. Was it Mira? No, she wouldn't be travelling with her ankle injured. Who then? He cocked his head. What was he doing here? Some niggling part of his brain said sheep, but that couldn't be right.

He excised himself from the strangling bed sheets and moved to the desk, hoping to find his journal and some clarity. But it wasn't to be found anywhere. Not on the desk, not in his things. He hadn't travelled without it, had he?

"You won't find anything there, chap."

Byron whirled towards a groggy Fred.

"Oh." He composed himself. "It's you."

Fred yawned. "Yeah, it's me. You forget again?"

"Unfortunately, yes. The only thing that comes to mind is sheep, but that can't be right."

A laugh escaped his partner as Fred stood and moved over to him. "No. It's right. Sheep and art thieves."

A half dozen images filtered through Byron's mind. "Art thieves. Right. We're going to the police today, aren't we?"

Fred grinned and clapped him on the back. "That's right! You remember now?"

"Mostly. You can fill me in on the way." Byron moved towards the door.

"Aren't you forgetting something?" Fred smirked and Byron turned back towards him.

"What?"

Fred gestured to his nightshirt.

"Oh. Right." Byron flushed and moved to actually get ready for the day.

Once they were both properly dressed and fed, they headed over to the Berkshire Constabulary. It was an unimposing building on the edge of a rather nice park in Reading. They entered and found a constable behind the desk.

"Good morning! What can I do for the two of you?" he said, all too cheery for the time of day.

"I'd like to report a crime." Fred leaned against the desk and said over his shoulder to Byron, "I've always wanted to do that."

Byron rolled his eyes. "It is true though. But we'd like to speak with the Chief Constable. We've been sent by Scotland Yard."

The constable's eyes widened. "Oh! The Home Office didn't say anything about this."

"Can we speak with the Chief Constable?" Byron asked.

"He's just in his office. Follow me."

The office was just down the hallway, and soon enough the constable knocked and disappeared behind the door. Byron could make out, "Yard," "I know, sir," and "Now," before the door opened again and the young constable ushered them inside. It was a cozy kind of office. A man with impressive mutton-chops and bushy eyebrows sat behind the desk.

"Good morning, gentlemen. I'm Colonel Adam Blandy, Chief Constable of the Berkshire Constabulary. May I ask who you are?"

"My name is Byron Constantine, and this is Frederick Wensley. Interim Commissioner Parry sent us."

The colonel's gaze sharpened. "Detective Constantine? From Palace Court?"

Byron cocked his head. "Yes? That would be me."

"I've followed your cases for years." Blandy held his hand out and Byron shook it. "It is a pleasure to meet you, sir. Please, sit down and tell me what I can help you with."

"We were originally sent to investigate that sheep panic you had a few days ago," Fred said, taking his seat.

"Ah yes." Blandy rubbed at his chin. "We've sent officers all over the county trying to figure out what happened. Best I can figure is that the lightning was particularly fierce."

"That is what we settled on as well," Byron said. "And then we stumbled onto some empty frames in a barn near Tidmarsh. After some investigating, we've determined that Berkshire has a couple of art thieves on the loose, and we decided to bring our findings to you."

"You aren't referring to the theft up at Taplow Court, are you?" Blandy leaned back in his chair.

"We weren't aware of that one, sir," Fred said. "But we have discovered thefts from Englefield House and Basildon Park. Four paintings in total."

"And another two from Taplow." Blandy rubbed at his temples. "This is more serious than I thought. We've been investigating the theft, of course, but it's been about a week and a half since it was reported and there hasn't been a breakthrough. Do you have any leads?"

Byron shook his head. "Nothing as of yet. We know that the thieves are posing as peddlers with the names Hugh and Liam Walter."

"Peddlers? And how do you know this?"

"The frames were in the loft of Harold Davies' barn. He allowed two peddlers to stay in that barn for a week. Not conclusive evidence, but it's a place to start," Byron said. "Do you have a map of the county handy?"

Blandy stood and moved over to a drawer, shuffled through some papers, and pulled out a large map, placing it on the desk.

Byron stood, eyes roving over the roads and landmarks. "Alright, here's Taplow Court. And you said the theft occurred over a week ago. Based on when the peddlers came to the Davies' farm, that would place the thefts at Englefield and Basildon after Taplow." He traced his finger from Taplow down to the other two estates. "Would they stop after three? Or move on to the next estate to the west?"

Blandy followed his line of sight. "That would be Shaw house. They don't have much in the way of an art collection. Not anything close to Basildon."

"Would the thieves know that?" Fred asked.

"Your guess is as good as mine." Blandy lowered himself into his chair. "What are you suggesting?"

Byron stood and paced in front of the desk. "We go to Shaw House and speak with the residents. With their permission, we set up a watch, and when the thieves show up, arrest them."

Blandy cocked his head to the side. "That might work, assuming they actually pull another heist. Worth a try at any rate."

They took a carriage this time, heading out to Shaw House with Colonel Blandy and one of his most trusted—and talkative—constables. Archibald "please call me Archie" Spurr was enlightening them on the difference between larch trees and other deciduous varieties, after a wholly riveting one-sided discussion about the efficacy of cheese. Fred was massaging his temples within the first five minutes of the ride. Likely because of how similar Archie was to Officer Jenkins back at Scotland Yard. As the young constable drew in a breath to switch the conversation once again, Blandy interrupted him.

"I say, Constantine, you never did tell me why the Yard sent you specifically to investigate this sheep nonsense. Or sent anyone at all, for that matter. It's certainly something we can handle on our own."

Byron let out a long breath. "Unfortunately, not everyone believes in my ability to solve cases. The new interim commissioner falls into that category, and he thought this would be a good test of my faculties."

Blandy's nose scrunched in disgust. "I would say your case history speaks to your abilities, well enough."

"Yes, but others are not quite as rational as you. Or are too rational to think that an amnesiac detective is within the realm of possibility."

The carriage trundled over a bump and the interior fell into blissful silence for the remainder of the ride. That is, until Archie asked if anyone had any jokes and proceeded to tell a slew of the most unfunny puns imaginable. A rush of gratitude fell over Byron when Shaw House came into view and they could finally cut the conversation short and get on to more interesting things.

They asked the driver to wait, and Byron led the way,

knocking on the door using a big brass knocker. Several minutes passed, and he knocked again. The door opened just a crack, and Byron made out a sliver of a man's face.

"I'm terribly sorry, but I can't open the door any wider at the moment. May I help you?"

"Er, yes. I believe so," Colonel Blandy said. "I'm Colonel Blandy, and this is Officer Spurr with the Berkshire Constabulary. And this is Detective Constantine and Officer Wensley with Scotland Yard. What was your name?"

"Henry Eyre. I'm—"

An indignant squawk and a flurry of rustling feathers cut the poor man off. He swore, leaving the door unattended.

"No! Bartholomew, get off of that clock! You stupid bird!"

Archie pushed the door open enough to slip through, and Byron and the others reluctantly followed behind, stopping in the main entry hall. The man, Henry, was standing at the base of a large grandfather clock, glaring up at an enormous blue bird.

"Robinson!" Henry yelled.

A butler appeared from a corridor. "Yes, sir?"

"Would you get a broom or something to get this blasted parrot down? And find out how he got out to begin with?"

Robinson nodded and disappeared.

Henry turned to the group. "I'm terribly sorry about all this. I can assure you that we normally don't have an overgrown pigeon terrorizing the place."

"He is not an overgrown pigeon!" A woman came into the hall, her blue walking dress sweeping around her feet.

Henry whirled on her. "It was *you*! You let the dirty thing out!"

"He looked so lonely there in the cage. Didn't you, Bartholomew?" She pulled a small piece of food from her pocket and raised it towards the parrot. Bartholomew lifted from his perch and alighted on her arm long enough to receive the proffered sustenance, then returned to his seat on the grandfather clock.

"If you don't keep that bird in that cage, I'll nail him there. I swear I will."

"Don't you listen to him, Bartholomew," she crooned to the bird. "He's just jealous."

"Jealous? Me? Of a bird?" Henry's nose crinkled.

"No. Of me. That I actually received something from our cousin, Frances."

"I bet she sent you that monstrosity," Henry gestured to Bartholomew, who was quietly preening himself on his ticking perch, "so she could be rid of the blasted thing."

Byron cleared his throat. It did nothing to draw the attention of the squabblers. With their similar build, facial features, and the method of their verbal attacks, they seemed to be siblings rather than spouses.

"What do you have against him anyway? He hasn't done anything to you."

"Hasn't done anything to . . ." Henry clenched his fists. "Bella, that villain has ruined four of my best shirts, pecked the living daylights out of me, and has made his best effort to be a nuisance in every conceivable way! And he only arrived this week!"

"This week!" the parrot repeated.

"And that's the other thing! The infernal beast keeps imitating me!"

"Well if you would just—"

"Henry. Isabella. Stop shouting this instant." An older woman appeared at the top of the grand staircase. Her wispy white hair was pulled into a bun, and she dressed in grey and lavender with accents of black. A mourning brooch kept her shawl in place. Byron made a mental note to express his condolences for her loss. As she swept down the stairs and into the entry hall, Henry and Isabella sobered and stepped away from each other.

"Sorry, Mama," Isabella said.

"Mama! Mama!" the parrot mimicked.

Their mother ignored the apology and the bird, turning instead to Byron and the others. "I must apologize for the behavior of my children. They should know better than to bicker in front of guests." She turned a glare onto the two of them. "Especially considering their age. Please, come with me to the parlor."

She turned to leave but stopped, saying, "Isabella, that bird had better be in its cage again when I return."

Leading the way into the parlor, she gestured for the group to be seated. She, for her part, took up an overstuffed armchair near the fire and pulled her shawl close around her shoulders.

"I do believe some introductions are in order, gentlemen."

"Of course." Colonel Blandy nodded and reintroduced each of them in turn.

The woman smiled. "You may call me Mrs. Eyre."

"Is there a Mr. Eyre that we could speak to?" Archie asked.

Byron held back a wince. The young constable needed to work on his observational skills.

The woman's gaze sharpened, a hand trailing to her brooch. "I'm afraid Mr. Eyre joined the choir invisible over a decade ago. He left me this house to live in with our children."

"How many children do you have?" Byron asked.

"Seven, living. You've met two of them. My two eldest, actually." She gave a long-suffering sigh that smoothed out into a smile. "You would think that after living in the same house for nigh on thirty years they would be able to put old griev-ances aside, but the smallest inconvenience pops up and they begin fighting like little ones again."

Byron chuckled. "I believe it happens to the best of us. And the parrot certainly doesn't help."

Mrs. Eyre softened at his tone. "No, it doesn't really. I don't know what got into Frances' head, sending it to us. She received that parrot as a gift years ago, and they got on quite well. But then she moved to Norway with her husband, and the poor thing is from the tropics. It became quite depressed." She shook her head. "But I doubt you came here to discuss parrots. How may I help you gentlemen?"

"We've come to ask if there have been any thefts from your estate in the last few weeks, or if there would be any art worth stealing," Fred asked.

Mrs. Eyre frowned. "Nothing has been stolen as far as I am aware. Why do you ask?"

"There have been a series of art thefts from Berkshire estates. Based on our estimates of the thieves' movements, Shaw House would be next." Byron once again found himself wishing for a pen and paper. He tapped his fingers against the armrest instead.

"I see." Mrs. Eyre adjusted her shawl. "That would explain yesterday's visitors, I believe."

"Yesterday's visitors?" Byron repeated.

"Yes. I'm afraid I don't know much about it, as I was in town posting some letters with Isabella. Mabel, my youngest daughter, was the only one at home. She told me upon my return that two peddlers had come by, asking for a tour of the house."

Byron shared a look with Fred.

"Did she give them one?" Fred asked.

"I believe she did. But she would know more on the subject." She reached over to a bell cord and pulled harshly on it. A few moments later, Robinson appeared in the doorway.

"Yes, madam?"

"Would you fetch Mabel for me, please? And bring some tea for our guests."

Robinson nodded and moved away.

"I should have thought about that to begin with." Mrs. Eyre

settled back into her seat. "Tea will be just the thing. Especially with the chill the air has taken on as of late."

"Tea would be splendid, Mrs. Eyre. Thank you," Colonel Blandy said.

A new woman, perhaps in her late twenties, came into the room in a hurry.

"You called for me, Mama?" Mabel said, giving a wary glance over the company.

"Yes, dear. Would you tell these detectives about the peddlers that came by yesterday?"

"Oh. Of course." Mabel took a seat next to her mother. "They came over around noon, or thereabouts. Mama and Bella were in town and Henry was out riding."

"Was anyone else in the house at the time?" Byron asked.

Mabel shook her head. "No one, except me. And the servants, of course. Robinson answered the door. They said that they had heard of Shaw House's incredible history and wondered if they could tour it. I had nothing better to do, and they seemed in earnest. We spent about an hour, Robinson and I, showing the public areas of the house."

"Were they interested in anything in particular?" Byron asked.

Mabel's brow furrowed. "Now that you ask, they were rather interested in the Constable. He kept remarking on how lovely it was."

"May we see this painting?" Colonel Blandy asked.

"Of course." Mrs. Eyre stood. "It's in one of the sitting rooms."

The group followed her to a sitting room where the painting hung above a fireplace. It was a lovely landscape piece displaying a forest and a river. The frame was about the same size as the ones they found in the Davies' barn.

"I can see why they fixated on it." Byron moved closer to it.

"It looks like half the paintings we passed in the hall," Archie mumbled.

Mrs. Eyre either didn't hear the remark or ignored it. "It was featured in the October 1884 Magazine of Art. Certainly the most expensive piece in our collection."

Byron frowned. "You wouldn't happen to have that issue, would you?"

"We have a bound edition in our library," Mabel said. "I can get it for you, if you wish."

"Please do."

As Mabel left the sitting room, Byron turned to Mrs. Eyre. "Did your family have any plans to be out of the area within the next week?"

"Tonight, actually. We've been invited up to Taplow Court by the Grenfells. We won't be back until Monday."

Colonel Blandy moved to stand next to Byron. "If the thieves are aware of that . . ."

"Yes, that would give them the perfect opportunity," Byron rubbed the back of his neck.

Mabel re-entered, bound edition in hand. "Here it is. I believe the page is marked." She set it on a side table and flipped to the correct page.

"May I?" Byron asked. Mabel pushed the book towards him. He skimmed through the article. "Here we are. It mentions Shaw House, Basildon Park, Englefield, and Taplow by name. Each with a pictured painting. It's focusing on art collectors in Berkshire."

Fred moved over and took the book. "By Jove, they've been using the magazine to plan where to hit. They can pick and choose anything they like just by reading this."

Archie frowned. "How can you be so sure?"

Colonel Blandy waved him off. "Miss Mabel, did you mention anything of your family's trip up to Taplow to those peddlers?"

"I don't believe I did. Although . . ." she trailed off in thought. "I may have told the parlor maid to get our trunks out so we could pack while they were in the entry hall." She bit her lip. "Actually, they did ask where we were going. Conversationally, of course, because I mentioned the trunks."

Byron turned to Mrs. Eyre. "The peddlers are the thieves we've been looking for, and based on what Mabel has told us, I believe they'll be attempting to steal this painting tonight."

"Then we will simply have to cancel our trip to Taplow and stay here."

Byron shook his head. "No, continue as you were. But with your permission, could we make use of this sitting room this evening?"

"Whatever for?"

Fred stepped forward. "To wait for the thieves, of course. If we're going to arrest them, and retrieve all the stolen paintings, we'll need to catch them in the act."

Mrs. Eyre paused for a moment, then nodded. "Make whatever arrangements you need."

November 11, 1888

THE GRANDFATHER CLOCK IN THE HALL STRUCK three. Byron shifted in his spot behind the folding screen. Fred sat next to him, stifling a yawn. Neither dared to speak in case the thieves decided to make an appearance. A sliver of moonlight trickled in through the curtains, illuminating the room.

The colonel and his constable had returned to the constabulary after the group had finalized the plan. The Eyre family left as they had previously intended. The remaining staff had all gone to sleep. And Byron and Fred were lying in wait, ready to follow the thieves back to where they held the rest of the stolen paintings, if possible. If not, they were ready to apprehend them. They had intended to set up shifts between them so that they could get some semblance of rest. Unfortunately, Fred snored, and Byron couldn't find any comfortable position on the floor, so the both of them had been up most of the night. On the floor between them was a paper filled with various scribbled messages and games visible only by the moonlight in the room.

A creak on the floor in the hallway had them both holding their breaths. The door opened.

"This is the one. Come on," a gruff voice said. The warmth of a lantern illuminated his figure through the screen. Tall and broad. A second figure joined the first. Just the opposite in build. The lantern shifted hands and the shadows disappeared as it was placed on the floor.

"What luck they were out, eh Dennis?" the shorter one said. "She'll be pleased that we retrieved the whole list."

"Shut up. There might still be servants up and about." The picture frame scraped against the wall as they pulled it down.

The short one hummed. "Then would it be better to take her off the frame here, or back at the cart?"

"Well, we—"

"Mama!" echoed through the hall and the thieves jolted, dropping the frame.

Fred stiffened beside Byron and gave him a questioning look. Byron lifted his hands and made a silent flapping motion. Fred's eyes widened with mirth, and he stifled a laugh. Luckily the thieves weren't paying attention enough to notice.

"Watch what you're doing!" Dennis hissed. "You'll damage it."

"But what was that?" the short one said. "You heard it didn't you?"

"I heard it, Monty. Must have been the wind. Now come on."

Byron filed both names away. Dennis and Monty. Could the latter be short for something? Montgomery? Monterey? Montague?

"Mama!" Another unsettling shriek rang out.

Byron winced at it. Bartholomew must have heard the thieves and thought the family had returned. Noisy bird.

"That's not wind," Monty said. "That's a child. And they wouldn't leave a child alone, would they?"

"What child sounds like that?"

Fred stifled another laugh, and Byron raised a hand to silence him, trying not to laugh himself. It wasn't a child, but rather an unruly parrot. But the thieves wouldn't know that.

"Mama!" No, to those who didn't recognize the sound of Bartholomew, it would sound more like the voice of a devil or something.

"Maybe it's not a child," Monty whispered, voice haunted. "Maybe it's the ghost of one."

"Don't be silly. Help me get this up."

"Can we just leave? She's not expecting this one."

"I'm not leaving it on account of your supersti—"

A booming crash interrupted them, startling all four men. Fred gestured to Byron, asking if it was time to make their presence known. Byron shook his head.

"What was that?" Monty said.

"Does it matter? Let's go. We'll take care of the frame later."

The light shifted as the thieves picked up the lantern and left the room. Byron leapt up to follow the dwindling light, Fred on his heels. They kept a fair distance from the thieves, quiet on their feet. And then the sudden beating of wings came as Bartholomew descended the staircase above them.

A shout from Monty punctuated another thud that sounded inside the lower sitting room. As Byron reached the door, a flurry of feathers and beak took over his vision. Claws gripped his arm as the parrot grappled him, moving up his shoulder and to his neck, wings flapping all the way, making it impossible to see or hear. Panic and fear rose inside him as he struggled with it. Eventually, he managed to get his hands up to where he could grab the bird and throw it off, running to the window.

"Blast!" He hit the windowsill. "They've gone."

Fred came in and surveyed the scene.

"You've killed it."

Byron whirled around, neck stinging. "No, I haven't."

The bundle of blue feathers stirred and hopped back up.

"See? Just stunned."

"Er. Right." Fred stepped around the bird as it flew to perch on an unfortunate armchair, its assault on Byron curtailed. Bird thus banished for the moment, they took stock of the room. The painting lay in a patch of moonlight, dropped in the thieves' haste to escape the demonic bird. Bartholomew, for his part, seemed unruffled, even as his feathers rustled in the slight breeze from the open window.

Rubbing his bleeding neck, Byron moved back to the window and closed it in case the bird wished to make its own exit.

"At least they left the painting." Fred picked up the frame and set it vertical against another chair.

"Mama!" Bartholomew squawked.

Byron glared at the bird. "Yes. But there are seven others that didn't have as good of a fate."

"Seven? I thought they only took two from each estate?"

Byron pointed to a bare spot on the wall. "There was a landscape there this morning. They must have stolen it before coming up for the Constable."

"Great. Now what?"

"Let's get some rest. Once the sun rises, we can search for clues."

"What about Bartholomew?"

"We'll deal with him in the morning. Come on."

Fred managed to track down some iodine to clean the cuts on Byron's face, neck, and shoulders. It did little to help and Byron tossed and turned in the bit of rest he got before sunrise.

The Eyre's had been kind enough to lend them some rooms for the evening, and Byron had never been so grateful to have a door with a lock on it. Not that he thought the bird would be able to navigate the handle, but he really didn't fancy the idea of another avian encounter.

He sat up, cuts stinging and limbs aching, and went about getting ready the best he could. His suit and shirt had gashes in them from the parrot's claws, but he put them on nonetheless and went to knock on Fred's door.

"Is it time already?" Fred yawned as he opened the door.

"Sun's up. And Blandy will be here in an hour or so. Best have something to go on."

"Oh, alright." Fred flattened his hair with his hand. "I'll be out in a bit."

Byron hovered outside the door for a few moments before going to investigate the crash from the night before. While he had his suspicions that a bird was involved, he wanted to make sure they weren't missing something. Sure enough, a few rooms down he found Bartholomew's cage, tipped on its side and wide open from the impact.

"It's a wonder he wasn't injured in the crash," Fred said, as he came around the corner.

"If he had been, maybe we'd have caught the thieves."

"You can't blame that on the bird, Byron."

"I can and I will." He crossed his arms.

"It was just a run of bad luck."

"In that case, why don't you try and get the bad luck back into its cage, and I'll go see if the thieves left any trace behind."

Fred grabbed his arm as he made to move past. "I think not, old chap. We're in this together, aren't we?"

"That was before you sided with the bird."

In the end, it took both of them, a broom, and a pickled herring they procured from the kitchen to get Bartholomew back into his cage. Having dealt with that, they had about thirty minutes left before the colonel was due to arrive. They started in the room with the Constable, going over the room for any footprints or papers that the thieves may have left behind. Finding nothing of consequence, they bundled up in their coats and headed outside, making their way around the side of the house to the window in question.

"They certainly left in a hurry," Fred said, examining how the shrubberies directly outside the window were damaged.

"Can you blame them?" Byron said.

Fred gave a noncommittal hum as Byron turned away from the window. The sun was starting to warm the frost on the grass, but the air was still quite frigid. Byron kept his hands in his pockets as he began to walk down toward the tree line. If they didn't find anything, they likely wouldn't find the thieves either. But he couldn't allow that outcome to take hold. If he didn't bring a case back to London, solved at that, there was no doubt that Durant would go free. And how could he face Mira again, knowing that? Perhaps he'd have to break Jack's confidence and explain that the panic had been an elaborate prank. But would solving a paltry sheep case be enough to keep his position with Scotland Yard?

"Hey, I found something. Think they might have dropped it?" Fred straightened from where he'd bent down to pick up a scrap of paper.

"What is it?"

"Looks like a ticket for the barge. It leaves tomorrow."

Byron furrowed his brow. "Barge? What barge?"

"The one the sheep are going on. Remember? The Davies' mentioned it the other day. Might have been dropped by anyone, come to think of it."

The missing memory slotted into place and an inkling came

to the forefront of Byron's mind. It finally made sense. "No. The thieves dropped it. In fact, they planned for it all along!"

"What do you mean?"

Byron clapped Fred on the shoulder and started moving up to the house. "I'll explain once the colonel gets here, but it seems the sheep are relevant after all!"

"What happened to your face?" Archie asked as Byron let him and the Colonel into the house.

Byron raised a hand to the scratch on his cheek. "An unfortunate run in with the bird. I'm glad both of you are here, though. I've got a plan for stopping the thieves."

"I'm glad you're here too," Fred said as they walked to the sitting room. "He refused to tell me what it was until you got here."

"I'll explain it. But first I need a piece of paper."

Blandy turned to Archie. "Have you got your notebook on you?"

Archie nodded and pulled it out, ripping a sheet from it and handing it to Byron.

"Thank you," Byron said, placing the paper on the table at the center of the room. "Fred, why don't you tell them what happened last night?"

He sketched a rough map of the area as Fred gave an account of the previous night's excitement.

"So, what's this plan of yours?" Blandy asked once he was apprised of the situation.

"First, what do we know about the thieves?" Byron capped his pen. "They're acting as peddlers, have a cart, and are generally working in a westward direction." He gestured to the map. "Based on what we overheard last night, they are working for someone else, a woman, and they've been using the Magazine of Art to plan which pieces to steal. We also know that initially they weren't planning on stealing anything from Shaw House. Now why would that be the case?"

Archie furrowed his brow. "They didn't think they could pull it off?"

"Why, though?" Byron asked. "They managed to steal from three other estates. What made this one so difficult?"

The room fell silent. Byron continued. "It wasn't a matter of difficulty, but rather a matter of timing." He fished around in his pocket and produced the barge ticket, setting it next to his map. "They dropped this last night in their haste to escape. A ticket that would get them on a barge to Bristol. But that barge was running late, wasn't it?"

"That's right," Fred said. "The owner stalled it so the farmers could get their sheep in order after the panic. It was originally going to leave on the eighth but they pushed it off to the twelfth."

"Which gave the thieves four extra days to work with," Byron said. "Four days wherein they could find another estate in the Magazine of Art, and steal another painting or two."

"But why would they take the barge at all?" Archie asked.

"Good question. After all, they do have their cart, don't they? They can take it wherever they want under the guise of peddling wares." Byron traced a possible path over the map with his finger. "However, that cart doesn't go very fast, and eventually they'll have to stop stealing paintings and start selling them. They can't sell them in Berkshire though. They'd have to go quite a bit away to sell their wares, otherwise once the thefts are reported, the police may catch up to them."

"So where are they selling them, Constantine?" Blandy asked.

"That, I can't say. But I would venture to guess that they'll be getting on a ship in Bristol that'll take them to their employer, wherever she may be."

Blandy nodded. "So, we head them off at the next stop. They'll have gotten on at Reading and relaxed some, and we can take a team on to arrest them."

Byron nodded. "That could work, certainly. There's only one issue with that."

"And what is that?" Archie asked.

"They still have an employer somewhere, and I doubt that they'll be willing to talk once we have them in custody. No, I think if we are to uncover the whole operation, we'll need to approach them on the barge itself. "

"What good will that do?" Blandy asked.

"If they think we are just fellow passengers, they'll be more likely to let things slip. Granted, we wouldn't want to over-crowd them. I'd suggest that Fred and I obtain passage on the barge and you arrange for a force to be waiting at the next stop to apprehend them."

Fred picked up the map. "I guess we just need to get a second ticket."

❦

That prospect was easier said than done. As it was a Sunday, it took some asking around to even find the owner of the barge. His house was up the hill from the dock and he'd just returned from church.

"Funny thing, I just had a man come round asking for a ticket. I gave him the last one."

"Who did you sell it to?" Byron asked.

Mr. Newman frowned and checked his papers, squinting at the writing. "Er. A Mr. Liam Walter?"

Byron nodded. "Is there any possibility that you could squeeze an extra passenger on?"

The man shook his head. "If we weren't hauling sheep, maybe. But as it is, we're full up."

"Thank you in any case," Byron said.

He returned to where Fred stood near the docks. "We're down a ticket, but the thieves are most certainly going to be on that barge tomorrow."

"So, which of us is going to go?" Fred asked. "Do we draw straws for it?"

"I'd rather not, honestly. There has to be some way we can both get on." Byron turned up towards the high street.

"We could say it was official police business. As it is."

"Yes, but could we trust that the workers wouldn't talk about us and reveal the whole thing? No. We need to keep this under wraps."

"I've got it!" Fred said. "They're loading sheep on it, aren't they? What if we just strap ourselves under the sheep? There's enough wool there we could hide amongst the throng."

"Nobody's going to believe that, Fred."

"Have you got a better idea?"

Byron stopped in the square. "Actually, I have."

For the second time in a week, they trekked through the mud that lined the path up to the Davies' farm. The wind shot through their coats as they approached the door. Byron noted that the cabbage looking bush was looking better. A dash of red sat at the tip of each of the green buds. Perhaps those buds were meant to turn into flowers? He shook his head and knocked on the door.

"Yer back?" Jack asked as he opened the door.

"Oh, mind your manners," Mrs. Davies called from further in. "Who is it?"

Mr. Davies shooed Jack away from the door. "It's those detectives from Scotland Yard, back again. How can we help ye gentlemen?"

"We wanted to speak with you about the barges. And more specifically about if we could help you with getting your sheep to Bristol."

Mr. Davies furrowed his brow. "Why would ye want to help me with that?"

Fred pulled his collar closer around his neck. "May we come in?"

"Surely ye can." Davies pulled the door wide so the two of them could enter. Jack had moved back to his seat at the table. He seemed a bit more at ease than he had the last time they'd met.

Mrs. Davies gestured to the extra chairs. "Take a seat, both of you. I'll get some tea going."

"That isn't necessary," Byron said. "We wouldn't want to trouble you."

"Although tea sounds wonderful," Fred said, rubbing his hands together.

Mr. Davies took a seat next to Jack. "Ye can't blame me for being suspicious of all this, after the strangeness with those peddlers."

"No sir, I understand," Byron said. "In fact, this has everything to do with the Walter brothers. We discovered why they wanted to stay in your barn, and I can assure you that they aren't peddlers whatsoever."

"Oh? What are they, then?" Mrs. Davies asked, bringing a dish of biscuits over to the table. Jack reached forward to take one and she shot him a look that had him leaning back again.

"Art thieves," Byron said.

"So that's it, then!" Jack's eyes lit up.

"That's what?" Mrs. Davies asked, cocking her head at her son.

"I saw into their cart on the first day, and all they had was a bunch of canisters. Not the kinds of things that a peddler would have to sell. I thought it strange at the time, but I had chores to do." He shrugged.

"Those canisters must have held the paintings," Fred said.

Byron nodded. "And they'll be using the sheep barge to bustle those paintings out of the country." He turned back to the Davies' family. "We've got one ticket ourselves, but we wondered if we could use Jack's ticket. We'd help you move the sheep, of course, and make sure they get to Bristol well enough."

"Oh, Jack's not going this year," Mrs. Davies said, back at the sink. "We couldn't afford a second ticket, so he'll be helping me out here. Won't you Jack?"

Jack looked less than pleased as he nodded. "Yes, Mum."

Fred sighed, turning to Mr. Davies. "And I'd guess you wouldn't be willing to give us your ticket with the good faith that we'd take care of the sheep?"

The man narrowed his eyes. "I'm not sure I fully trust the situation enough to send my livelihood off with ye. After all, ye could be the thieves."

"Harold!" Mrs. Davies scolded. "You can't go throwing around accusations."

"He's quite right to question us," Byron said. "There's no way for us to prove our good intent."

"And aside from that" —Fred grabbed a biscuit— "We know little to nothing about handling sheep."

Byron sighed. "Which leaves us in an unfortunate place when it comes to the art thieves."

"Now hold on there," Mr. Davies said. "Why don't ye start from the beginning?"

Byron shared a look with Fred before delving into the details of the investigation. When he was done, Harold Davies leaned back in his chair, sipping at his tea with a thoughtful expression.

"Aye, I think I can help ye."

"So, you'll give us your ticket?" Fred asked.

"I didn't say that. But I can help." He set his teacup down.

"The way I see it, ye only need one of you on the barge. But if yer wanting to keep the thieves out of the know, you'll need an excuse to be there, won't ye?"

"Yes?" Byron leaned against the table.

"There'll be men from 'cross the county who'll all know me. They'll know ye aren't from round here and question you. But we could avoid all that if ye came with me. We could say ye were my cousin or something thereabout. We can twist up some story about Jack being sick so folks won't question his whereabouts. You'll help me get the sheep on the barge, and from there you'll be able to find those Walter brothers. What say ye?"

Byron turned to Fred. "I suppose we just need to decide which one of us will go."

Fred pulled some straw from his pocket, with a grin. "Good thing I grabbed this on the way in."

November 12, 1888: Morning

"You alright there, chap?" Fred asked the next morning as Byron readied himself to go to the Davies.

"Just tired, that's all."

The sun hadn't come up yet and Byron couldn't shake the feeling that he was forgetting something. His blasted brain was acting like a sieve again. And without his journal, there was no way to know other than to trust Fred to remind him. Maybe leaving it behind was a mistake.

"Actually." He sighed. If he forgot something for the case, it was better to be honest with Fred and get the facts. "Remind me of the plan? I don't want to forget anything."

Fred nodded. "I'll be meeting up with Colonel Blandy and his people first thing this morning. We'll head off to the Newbury port, down by the Kennet. The barge should get there around midday, where we'll arrest the thieves and retrieve the stolen goods. That means you and Harold will only have a few scant hours to find out who hired them and where they were taking the art."

"Right. And only after we've settled the sheep in."

"See, you remember."

Byron shook his head. "I still feel like I'm missing something. Something important."

"It'll come to you. Now you ought to get going. The sooner you leave the longer you'll have on the barge."

Byron continued to puzzle over his lost memories as he walked up to the Davies farm. Was it something to do with the case? Or something else entirely? He paused at the door to appraise the bush just outside. The buds no longer looked like cabbages. In fact, the red tinge had spread and opened a bit, revealing that they were indeed flowers. What might they look like in full bloom?

He knocked on the door and Mrs. Davies answered.

"Have ye had breakfast yet?" she asked.

"Oh, I have. Thank you, though."

She led the way into the kitchen. Jack waved from where he sat at the table, eating porridge.

"Harold is just coming down now." She furrowed her brow. "That's not what you're wearing, is it?"

Byron glanced at his attire. "It isn't ideal for the situation, I know, but I didn't anticipate needing a disguise."

"I bet you'll fit in some of Harold's old clothes. I won't be a moment!" She stepped out of the room just as Harold came in, wiping off his hands.

"Now what's she up to, I wonder?" He laughed. "Are ye ready to go, Mr. Constantine?"

"Not quite. I believe your wife is scrounging up a disguise for me. And we probably ought to get our story straight too."

"Ah yes. Well, most people know I've got some extended family out of Brighton. Last name Simmons."

Byron hummed. "What do you think of the name Eric to go with it?"

"Eric Simmons." Jack nodded. "It's got a good sound to it. Don't reckon we've got a cousin with that name though."

"It'll do fine," Mr. Davies said, heading out the door. "I'll just go call Bruce and we can get going once you're ready."

Byron turned to Jack. "Bruce isn't one of the sheep, is he?"

The younger boy laughed. "No. Dad makes it a practice not to name the sheep. You get attached you see. That is if you can remember which is which."

A short whistle sounded from outside and Byron stepped through the door. An enormous shaggy dog shuffled up to Mr. Davies. "Morning, Bruce," he said, giving the dog's head a ruffle and looking up at Byron. "Bruce here is the best herding dog I've ever had."

Byron frowned. The dog's fur was all up in his eyes. How could such a beast *see* the sheep, let alone herd them?

Mrs. Davies came to the doorway, arms laden with clothing. "Try some of these on and see if they don't fit, Mr. Simmons."

❦

Soon enough Byron looked the part, and he and Harold Davies set off with the sheep. Luckily, they weren't taking the whole flock, just about a dozen. They'd already been shorn and separated into their own pen. And on the road Byron didn't need to do much as Harold and his dog kept the flock together well enough on their own.

"You really didn't need my help, did you?" he said as they came into town.

"Oh no, Eric. You've been a great help in terms of company. I usually have Jack around to make conversation. And besides, you've got to learn the business somehow."

Byron smiled to himself. It seemed that Harold was having more fun with the ruse than he realized. All the way along, regardless of whether anyone was within hearing range, the man had been acting like Byron truly was his cousin.

There was one other herdsman with about ten sheep once they got to the river. He and Harold didn't seem too worried about their sheep mixing as they waited their turn to be herded onto the barge. Harold, seeing his confusion, leaned over and said, "We've all tagged them in the ears, see?" He pointed to the closest ewe, and upon closer inspection Byron found a metal tag on the ear. "We're all going to the same place and they'll be mixed together at one point or another. Doesn't matter none when it happens."

In a slow trickle they managed to get all the sheep into the barge and into the makeshift paddocks onboard. While Harold directed Bruce to watch the sheep on the deck, Byron caught sight of a faded yellow peddler's cart on the aft side of the barge.

"Hello there, Harold. Who's that with you there?" The other herdsmen tipped his hat to them as they came on deck.

"This is my cousin, Eric Simmons, from Brighton. He's up to help us winter everything down."

"Ah. A pleasure there, Eric. I'm Tom Chapman." He offered his hand and Byron shook it.

"Pleased to be here, sir," Byron matched their inflections. "Haven't had much experience with sheep up to now."

Tom laughed. "You'll get there soon enough, lad."

Two men, presumably part of the crew, pulled the loading boards onto the deck. A mule was attached to the barge at the front and would pull the barge upstream while the third member of the crew walked alongside it on the towpath. Tom clapped a hand on Harold's shoulder. "Come on now, there's an enclosed area there at the front. I'll talk to the captain and be right down."

Byron and Harold bustled down a short staircase at the front of the barge and down into a lower level, stooping to avoid hitting their heads on the struts that supported the canvas covering. As they came around the corner, they heard whispers coming from ahead of them. Byron gestured for Harold to stop and listen.

"Miss Vermielle will be pleased we got that last one, eh Dennis?" Monty said.

"Keep it down. The whole ship'll know if you keep yapping like that."

"Oh, there's no harm in it. Who's around to hear? The sheep?"

"Those farmers'll come down at some point."

Vermielle. The name seemed familiar, but Byron couldn't pin it on anything. It wasn't a common surname, that was certain.

"Good news," Tom Chapman bellowed as he came down the staircase himself. The thieves went quiet. "They've got a man going on ahead to prep the locks. Should cut an hour off the first leg of the trip."

"Glad to hear it," Harold said, coming fully around the corner.

They came to a small seating area designed for those transferring cargo but not necessarily working or living on the barge. The thieves were sitting on the far side, eyes widened in panic as they approached. At first, Byron thought it was because they were worried they'd been overheard. But their gaze was set on Harold.

"Mr. Davies!" the taller one said. "I'm so glad you're here."

"Are ye, now?" Harold narrowed his eyes.

"Yes, we've been meaning to apologize. Haven't we, Liam?" He nudged the shorter one with his elbow. Byron took note of the healing wound on Liam's face. Similar to the one he himself had received from the parrot. That man had to be Monty then.

"Oh yes, sir!" Monty said, nodding his head. "We just didn't think we'd get the chance to explain ourselves."

Harold crossed his arms. "And what sort of explanation could you have?"

The thieves shared a look, the taller one stuttering for an answer.

Harold put them out of their misery. "I mean, I'm sure you had some very important peddling to be getting on with, but not even bothering to say goodbye? Mrs. Davies was quite put out that she couldn't feed you breakfast," he teased.

The thieves broke into nervous laughter.

"We are rightly sorry about all that, 'specially after you were so nice as to put us up for those few nights," Monty said. "But it's as you said. We realized we were behind on our sales and had to get a move on."

Harold shook his head. "It's no matter. You helped me realize that I needed some more help with things. That's why I brought my cousin up from Brighton." He turned to Byron. "Eric, this is Hugh and Liam Walter. And this is Eric." He gestured to the relevant parties and moved to take a seat across from the thieves.

"A pleasure to meet you both," Byron said, sitting next to Harold. Tom opted to stand near the entryway.

"What happened to Jack?" the Dennis in Hugh's clothing asked, narrowing his gaze at Byron. "I'd have thought you would have brought your son instead of sending for a cousin."

"Oh, he came down with a fever real sudden," Harold said. "And we were already having Eric come up to help get things settled for the winter."

This seemed to appease Dennis for the moment.

"You say you're both peddlers?" Byron asked, testing the waters.

"Aye," Dennis said. "Been in the business a few years."

Byron nodded. "What sorts of things do you sell?"

"All sorts," Monty said. "Pots, pans, linens, fine china, encyclopedias, whatever we happen to come across. Rarities from 'round the world."

Tom whistled. "Must do a fair bit of travelling then. Where's the furthest you've ever gone?"

Dennis hesitated. "Spain, I'd say."

"Incredible," Byron said. "Is that where you're off to now?"

"No, we're going to France," Monty said.

Dennis jabbed his elbow into Monty's side and he amended, "Well, actually Bristol. France won't be for a few months."

Byron nodded. "I've always wanted to travel."

"Ever been to Bristol?" Tom asked.

Byron shook his head and frowned. Some memory was tickling at the back of his mind. Faint. Had he been to Bristol?

The group fell into moderate silence as the barge began to move. The thieves whispered between themselves, and Tom took a seat and pulled out some tools for whittling, puffing on a pipe every few minutes. Most of the trip continued in this way. A few conversations here and there, particularly while the barge was going through the locks.

The silence didn't help Byron to remember. In fact, it felt a bit stifling. His pulse and breath quickened, being confined to such a small space. About an hour into the trip, he stood. "I'm going to go up top, if that's alright." He looked to Harold, who inclined his head.

He followed the short path back to where the sheep were held. The chill air rushed at him as he left the warmth of the enclosed area, and he pulled his collar tighter around his neck. The barge was making good time along the river. Likely only a few more hours before it would reach Newbury, if the locks were clear.

The sheep bleated here and there from their paddocks and a worker stood where he could see the whole barge. Byron moved to the side and took a few deep breaths. He'd been doing so well, at least from what he could tell. Remembering most everything from day to day. He curled his hands over the metal railing, the coolness of it grounding him as he watched the wake of the barge in the water.

"You alright there, mate?"

Byron startled, turning towards the shorter of the thieves. Monty or Liam depending on which was the true moniker. He hadn't even heard him approach.

"Oh. Fine. Just not used to enclosed spaces is all. Never been on a barge before." Or had he? How much had he entirely forgotten from the past few years? He'd been meaning to read through all of his journals and get all the facts since his memory retention had improved.

"I understand." Monty nodded. "Have you always wanted to be involved with sheep?"

"Not really, no. But it's the family business, and it's not like I could do much else."

"I understand that. My father wanted me to enlist with the regiment."

"Did you?" Byron filed that information away.

Monty shifted on his feet, uncomfortable. "Well, I'm a peddler now."

The army was an uncomfortable topic then. Interesting. Byron took pity on the man and pointed towards the faded yellow cart. "Is that yours, then?"

Monty leaned out over the railing. "Yup. Needs a bit of paint, but it's sturdy."

"Peddling's a good job for you then?"

"Good enough." Monty sighed. "Sometimes I wish it weren't necessary."

"It's a living though?" Byron said.

Monty hummed to the affirmative, and they settled into silence again, other than the rustling and baaing of the sheep.

"I couldn't help but overhear earlier . . ."

"Yeah?" Monty's eyes narrowed.

"You mentioned someone named Vermielle. Are they your merchant for your goods?"

"Oh." Monty ran a hand over his chin. "Yeah. She's our, er, merchant."

"Vermielle." Byron tested the name out again. Why was it so familiar? "That's French, right?"

"As far as I know, yeah. She's in France at any rate."

Byron nodded. "Must be nice to travel so much."

"You get used to it after a while. Loses its interest when you've been on so many boats."

"If you could do anything else, what would you do?"

"An interesting question, that. I'm not sure I'd know." He fell silent for a moment. "Truth be told, we used to be in the regiment." There was an undertone of guilt in his voice.

"Is that so?" Byron would wager that the two thieves had deserted. That would explain why the two of them had resorted to crime.

Monty leaned farther over the edge. "Not sure why I'm telling you this." He lifted his head up, a considering look on his face. "You just seem trustworthy."

"I won't tell anyone." The constabulary was certain to find out eventually, but Byron wouldn't hurry that process along. Desertion was often a crime punishable by death.

Monty relaxed. "You ever consider peddling, Eric?"

Byron frowned at the sudden change of subject. "Never given it much thought before. Why?"

"When we get to Bristol, we were planning on selling the cart, see? And if you were interested, I'd be willing to give you a discount on it."

"Selling the cart? Why?"

"Oh, well," Monty leaned in closer. "I'll let you in on another secret. We *are* going to France straightway. We've traded some things that our merchant may be interested in, and we need to get them there as soon as possible. It's harder to travel with a cart. And we can get a new one easily enough."

"I'd have to think about it. Peddling could be an interesting occupation. Much different than sheep."

"It would be, yes. But you've got time to think before we get to Bristol." Monty stretched his back. "I'm going to head back down. It's a bit chilly up here."

"Aye. It is. I'll follow you back down."

About three hours into the trip, the group broke out their packs for lunch and the conversation picked up again.

"I'll tell ya, those sheep were a right nuisance to get rounded up again after that storm. Real messy business, that," Tom Chapman said.

"We heard about it after the fact," Dennis said. "That's part of the reason I feel so rotten about leaving when we did. If we'd just stayed on another night or so we could have helped you and your boy set everything to rights."

"Oh, don't bother yourself about it. What's done is done," Harold said, leaning back.

"It may be done, but it's still a strange thing. Still can't figure how it happened," Chapman said around a mouthful of sandwich before continuing. "Speaking of strange, have you heard anything more from those detectives of yours?"

Byron tensed at the question and glanced at Harold who shrugged.

"Er. Detectives?" Monty asked.

"Oh yes, tell em Harold," Chapman said.

"There's not much to tell, all told," Harold said, gaze set on his lunch.

"Sure, there is." Chapman turned to the thieves. "Just a few nights ago he comes into the pub all excited. Says he's had detectives up from Scotland Yard asking him questions about what else? Sheep. All this pomp and nonsense over that panic."

"Really?" Dennis asked. "What kind of questions did they ask?"

"Oh, nothing much. Not really," Harold said. "Asked about what the night was like. Where the sheep ran off to. That sort of thing."

"Didn't you say they were interested in your barn?" Chapman asked.

Byron wished the man would stop talking.

"Yes, but they didn't find anything. Thought maybe something about the barn was what spooked the sheep. Makes no sense, seeing as all the sheep in the county startled simultaneously."

"But they searched it?" Dennis asked.

"Aye."

Dennis' brow furrowed and he shared a look with Monty. "Let's head up and check on the cargo. Make sure it hasn't jostled any."

"Right." Monty stood, and the two of them disappeared around the bend and up the staircase.

Chapman frowned. "Odd pair, those two. Never seen peddlers take a livestock barge before."

"They are a bit strange, aren't they?" Harold said. "They said they were going all the way to Bristol?"

"Aye," Chapman said. "We're making a good clip. Ought to make it to Marlborough in the late afternoon. Not sure where we'll stop for the night."

"Marlborough?" Byron asked. "I thought the next stop was Newbury?"

"It would have been, had any tickets been bought there. I was talking with the captain 'fore we got moving. We've only got a few stops this time, other than the locks."

Byron let out a slow breath. There wouldn't be a police force waiting in Marlborough. And there was no way to communicate with Fred or Colonel Blandy that the plans had changed.

Harold set his lunch sack aside, picking up some meat he'd left alone "I'm going to go check on Bruce. Do you want to come with me, Eric?"

Byron nodded and stood with him, heading back to the stairs. Harold gave a short whistle once they came to the top, and Bruce came lolloping over. Bending down, Harold broke off a piece of the meat and offered it to the dog.

"Yer people are out in Newbury, aren't they?"

Byron nodded. "Yes. Which makes things rather tricky. We haven't passed Newbury yet, as far as I can tell. We have to get the barge to stop somehow."

"Aye, I see the issue." Harold stood, giving his dog a pat. He narrowed his eyes. "I wonder what they're up to."

Byron followed his line of sight over to the thieves. It was difficult to see exactly what they were up to with all the sheep in the way, but he could make out that the back of the covered cart was open. Monty was leaning over the back railing quite a ways, Hugh handing something to him.

"That is rather odd, isn't it?" Byron furrowed his brow.

"Must have dropped something to be leaning over the side like that," Harold said, turning back to face the shore. "They're lucky he dropped it there, otherwise it would be long gone."

Byron kept his sights on the thieves, noting that as Monty came back up he didn't have anything in his hands. "Why is that?"

"There's a dinghy off the back there. Higher chance for it to fall in it than in the water."

"Ah. Definitely lucky for him then."

The barge moved up and down in line with the ripples in the water. Byron continued to keep an eye on the thieves through the hooves and wool. If they were offloading the paintings to the dinghy, there was a possibility they'd break away before the barge even reached Bristol. Chapman's talk of detectives must have spooked them.

He cocked his head. "The sheep seem to be taking to the water well enough."

"It's just a floating paddock to them."

"Still, not a lot of room for them."

"Aye. I suppose." Harold surveyed the sheep and lowered his voice. "Do you have a plan?"

"The beginnings of one." Byron nodded towards the cart at the back. "First, I need you to distract them. If you're right about the dinghy, I need to check to see if the stolen goods are there."

"Ah! I knew there was something off about you!" Chapman said, coming up the stairs. "Yer the detective!"

Byron's eyes grew wide as Harold crossed over to the stairs. "Hush now, don't be yelling it out for everyone," Harold said.

"I'm right though, aren't I?" Chapman grinned, showing his tobacco-stained teeth.

"How did you know?" Byron said, checking to make sure the thieves were out of earshot.

"Truth be told, I didn't know for certain till you mentioned stolen goods just now. But I know most of Harold's cousins, and you don't have the right coloring for them. What's brought you to the barge?"

"Art thieves," Harold said. "And you'd best keep your mouth shut about it."

"Never say that Thomas Chapman can't keep a secret. But I'd like to help."

Byron nodded. "Alright then. This has two parts to it. First, I need to see what they've been doing back there. That'll require keeping them in the front of the barge for at least five minutes."

"That'll be simple enough." Tom said. "What else?"

Byron cocked his head from side to side. "How well do you two know sheep?"

Harold laughed. "I was raised with 'em. I reckon I know more about sheep than you do about detecting."

"You may be right, but answer me this: how does one spook a sheep?"

Harold paused for a moment, brow furrowing. "A fair question, that. There are a few ways I can think of. What are ye intending?"

Byron's eyes traced the shoreline. "Can sheep swim?"

Chapman frowned. "Only if they have to, and if it isn't a far distance."

"Good. We need to get this barge to stop at Newbury, or before. Otherwise, the police won't be able to arrest them. Can either of you tell where we are right now?"

Harold studied the scenery. "Well, we most recently passed the Monkey Marsh Lock."

"No," Tom interrupted. "We passed that back in That-cham. The last one was Widmead."

"Ah, that's right," Harold said. "In that case we're about ten minutes out."

Byron nodded. "I'll ask the captain if we can stop first, but if not, I'll need a diversion. Something that would force the barge to stop."

"Like the sheep panicking. I see." Harold sighed. "If we're careful about it we won't hurt the stock."

"Aye." Chapman scratched at his stubble and took another puff of his pipe.

The group quieted as the thieves moved around the sheep towards the front again. The two stopped to talk to the captain and the workman. Hugh pulled something out of his pocket and handed it over to the captain. Byron frowned, but kept quiet as the thieves continued their trek around and approached them.

"Is something wrong?" Dennis asked.

"Just wanting to check on the sheep, and on Bruce here." Harold scratched the dog behind his ear.

Satisfied, Dennis nodded and headed towards the staircase. Monty stopped to pet the dog before following his partner in crime to the front. Byron moved over to the far railing, the farmers right behind him.

"Did either of you see what they handed the captain?"

"Hard to tell," Chapman said. "Looked to be money."

"I was afraid of that. I'll try to talk to the captain and check for the goods. If I'm not back in seven minutes, I need you to startle the sheep. Keep those two busy at the front if you can."

Harold nodded. "We'll be sure to keep them occupied. You can tell the story about the ewe that fell in your well."

Chapman smiled. "Aye, that'll work."

November 12, 1888: Afternoon

THE TWO FARMERS HEADED DOWN THE STAIRS, and Byron moved towards the captain and workman. They seemed to be finishing a conversation, and as he approached, the workman moved away.

"Excuse me," Byron said. "I just heard that we won't be stopping in Newbury."

"Aye, that's right," the captain said. "There isn't a reason to."

"Would it be possible to stop in any case?"

He shook his head. "If we do, we'll be behind schedule and our lock man may prep the lock too early, causing issues for the other barges."

"Aye, that makes sense," Byron said. "What were the Walter brothers saying to you just now?"

The captain averted his gaze. "It's not your business, is it?"

"I suppose not. Good day to you."

Byron moved around the side of the barge, being careful to avoid any mess on the deck left by the sheep. He came to where the covered cart stood, yellow paint peeling to reveal the sun-bleached wood underneath. A padlock kept the back doors closed, but that suited him just fine. He came up to the back railing and leaned over. Sure enough, there was the dinghy, trailing behind by a short bit of rope. Inside were several canisters that could easily hold rolled up canvases. Seven, to be precise.

A hand grabbed his shoulder and wrenched him back, keeping a firm grip as they turned him around.

"What are you doing?" Dennis asked, voice gruff and eyes dangerous. Monty stood behind him, eyes wide.

"I was looking at your cart." Byron thought fast, cataloguing Dennis' strength. "Liam mentioned you might be selling it. But it looks like something's fallen in the dinghy back there. "

"You should keep your nosing to yourself," Dennis pushed him against the railing, hand fisted in Byron's collar.

"He wasn't hurting nothing," Monty said.

"He's poking about where he shouldn't."

Byron cleared his throat. "Sorry, I didn't realize those canisters were yours."

Dennis just glared.

Byron swallowed. "Right. Can you let go then?"

Dennis' hand tightened on his collar. "I think there's something strange about you. Tell us exactly why you were snooping."

"It's like I said, honest! If they mean that much—"

A round of intense barking rang out from the front of the ship. The three men whipped their heads in that direction. The sheep-dog, Bruce, had his paws up on the edge of a paddock and continued to bark incessantly. A wave of unease and turmoil rolled through the sheep. The deck of the barge undulated with wool and hooves as the sheep panicked with no place to go. The wood creaked and groaned against the movement.

Byron took a step back as one of the paddocks splintered and broke apart, sheep hurling themselves off of the edge of the barge and plummeting into the water. Harold waved from where he stood at the front of the barge, much too pleased with himself. Monty grabbed hold of the yellow cart as the sheep pushed past him and into Byron and Dennis. As the barrage of fleece barreled into him, Byron's feet flew over his head and he went tumbling off the barge.

The water came too fast and too cold, rushing through his ears as he tried to orient himself. He circled his arms around, trying to get to the surface while the water seeped into his woolen clothes, pulling him down. He tugged at the sleeves of his coat, pulling it off and letting it sink to the bottom of the canal. Something thrashed beside him as he finally righted himself and came to the surface, sputtering.

Managing to swim to the side of the dinghy, he latched onto it and coughed as he caught his breath. The muffled sounds around him turned into shouts and bleats as the water receded from his ears.

"Dennis!" Monty called from the deck of the barge. "He's fallen in! He can't swim!"

Byron turned to where Dennis thrashed under the water. He dove over and grabbed the man under his arms, pulling him back to the surface and over to the dinghy. He sputtered and coughed as Byron guided his hands to the side of the boat. Around them, a half dozen sheep thrashed as they swam towards the shore.

"Grab the paddles! We need to stop the barge!" the captain yelled.

Slow and steady, the barge stopped next to the shore. Byron let out a sigh of relief. They'd stopped the barge. Now he just needed to get back on, get into town and bring Blandy and Fred down to where they were moored. The two farmers could keep the thieves busy that long, couldn't they?

Bracing himself against the edge of the dinghy, he hoisted himself up and over the edge. He moved the canisters out of the way and then helped Dennis up. The wind swept around them, and he resisted the urge to shiver as they sat in the bottom of the boat.

"You saved my life," Dennis said, voice hoarse as he took a few shaky breaths.

"Don't mention it." Byron coughed. "Never seen anything quite like that." He combed a hand through his hair, pressing the water out. "We ought to row into shore. Maybe see if we can help with the sheep."

Dennis looked up at Monty. "Come on down and we'll get off here."

Monty nodded and maneuvered his way down. The dinghy shook as he landed in the bottom of it. Byron braced himself inside it, not wanting to be tipped out. He and Dennis each took a hold of one of the paddles and started to guide the dinghy towards the dock where a crowd had gathered. Either that, or the police force was already waiting. Byron hoped it was the latter.

They brought the dinghy up to the bank and clambered out. Dennis handed Monty the stack of cylindrical canisters before he hopped onto the bank as well.

"We ought to go up to that dock over there," Monty said. "The barge will probably moor there before continuing after they get the sheep."

"Good plan," Dennis said.

"Do you want some help with those?" Byron asked, reaching for the canisters.

"Why, thank you!"

Monty started to hand them over but Dennis took them before he could. "We've got it handled. Thanks."

Byron shrugged and continued to walk, shivering in the autumnal wind.

They came up to the dock, and Byron smiled to see Fred and Blandy among the throng that awaited them. Fred caught sight of him and came over.

"Whatever happened to you lot?"

Byron laughed. "A bit of a dip in the Kennett. Allow me to introduce my friends. This is Hugh and Liam Walter."

Dennis gave a sharp nod. Monty waved.

"This your friend, Eric?" Monty asked.

"Yes, actually. Allow me to introduce Frederick Wensley of Scotland Yard and Colonel Blandy of the Berkshire Constabulary."

Confusion crossed both of the thieves' faces before Dennis threw the painting canisters at Monty and ran down the dock. Monty scrambled to keep hold of them, several of them rolling down the bank towards the water.

Byron sprinted through the crowd, weaving in and out of people as he kept sight of Dennis. The thief, for his part, darted into the town square and down an alleyway. Byron matched him step for step until they came to a fence between the buildings that blocked the way.

Dennis turned and pulled out a knife. "I knew there was something fishy about you from the moment I saw you. You aren't even from around here, are ya?"

"Neither are you, Dennis. Why don't you put the knife away and we'll talk?"

"No, you'll let me go right now or else I slit your throat right here."

"With the police just around the corner? Come now, Dennis. You don't want to add a murder charge on top of theft and desertion."

That was evidently the wrong thing to say as the thief's shoulders tightened. "What'd you just say?"

"Desertion. I understand why you might turn to crime rather than be caught. Stealing for Miss Vermielle is likely more profitable, and less risky, than fighting in Egypt."

"What do you know?"

"More than you might think. Just put the knife away. I'm sure the Berkshire Constabulary would love to work something out with you and Monty if you just cooperate."

Dennis' eyes darted from side to side, his entire body tense as he looked for an exit. Based on his movements, Byron estimated it would take about fifteen seconds or less for Dennis to either surrender or fight.

Fourteen seconds.

Thirteen.

Dennis shifted to the left and Byron ducked to the ground, picking up some sand as the thief rushed him. He threw the sand in Dennis' eyes and stepped aside. Dennis flinched back at the sand, wildly slashing the knife in the air. Byron stepped forward and grabbed the wrist holding the knife, twisting it behind Dennis' back.

"Drop the knife, please." Byron kept a firm grip on his arm as Dennis writhed and tried to get out of the hold. The knife slipped from his grasp, and Byron kicked it away.

Fred ran into the alley, and Byron let out a breath of relief. "Please tell me you have handcuffs on you?"

"Blandy does. He's currently supervising the retrieval of the paintings. Several fell into the river and started floating away."

"Course they did." Byron sighed. "Would you grab that knife then and help me get him over there?"

Fred did as he was asked and grabbed Dennis' other arm. "Come on, then."

When they got back to the dock, Archie's arms were laden

with dripping canisters and Monty was kneeling, handcuffed, on the dock next to a soaking wet sheep. Blandy pulled out another set of cuffs and set about restraining Dennis.

"Good work. Did you get the information we were looking for?" Blandy asked.

"I did. Actually I—"

"Eric? You're the detective?" Monty asked, dumbfounded.

"Byron Constantine, at your service." He nodded to him before turning back to Blandy. "Miss Vermielle is their contact in France."

"Vermielle?" Fred's eyes widened. "You mean that burglar that was terrorizing north London a few months ago?"

Byron snapped his fingers. "I thought the name sounded familiar!"

"She's part of the reason you solved the Pennington case. You and Thatcher let her go because of it."

"I trusted you!" Monty said, fists clenching in his cuffs and face turning red. Byron could tell part of his anger came from the realization that he'd confided in the wrong person. The sheep next to him bleated.

"I am sorry, really I am," Byron said. "But I'm sure if you work with the constabulary they'll be lenient. Isn't that right, Colonel?"

"Generally, that is the case," Blandy said, then turned to Fred and Byron.

"Come around to the constabulary when you get a moment. I'll write something up for you to take back to Scotland Yard. I think with this under your belt, there's no possibility of them denying your abilities now."

"I suppose we'll see when we get back," Byron said. Parry was still a wildcard. There was always the possibility he'd find some other way of complicating matters.

Blandy nodded to the both of them before he and his constables pulled the thieves to standing and started moving them and the paintings towards the police wagon.

"Well. That's that, then." Fred handed the knife over to Byron. "I'm glad things worked out."

"I am too. Although I'd prefer that I didn't take a swim." Byron rubbed at his arms as the wind picked up.

"Yes, we ought to get you dry. You look like a drowned sheep."

"I certainly feel like one."

Harold approached them, his dog at his side. "We've taken account of all the sheep. None were injured. Did ye catch them?"

"We managed, yes. Thank you for your help. I'm not sure I would have been able to stop the barge by myself." Byron reached his hand out and Harold shook it.

"'Twas a pleasure. I'd do it again if I could." He took a step back. "Would the two of ye mind doing a favor for me?"

"Not at all. What can we help you with?"

"Well, with all this excitement, I'm sure my missus will hear something about it. News does travel and whatnot during the markets. Could ye go and let Martha and Jack know that I'm alright, and so are the sheep? I'd do it meself, but the captain wants to keep going as soon as we get the sheep back onboard."

"Of course." Byron smiled.

After drying off and enjoying a bracing cup of tea in the pub, the two headed out to the Davies farm for the last time. The sun was starting to set by the time they reached the door, curious sheep following behind them. The buds on the bush outside the door had bloomed in beautiful shades of pink. Byron stopped to smell them before knocking on the door, only slightly disappointed that the flowers didn't have a scent. Martha opened the door for them a moment later.

"Ah! Mr. Constantine and Mr. Wensley. Did everything go alright?"

"It went quite well, all things considered. I'm afraid I lost your husband's coat in the river, though," Byron said as Martha ushered the two of them in. "I'd like to replace it, if possible."

"Oh, that's most kind of ye, but you needn't bother. It wasn't his size anymore in any case. Did you want your clothes back?"

"Thank you, that would be great."

"Jack!" she called further into the house.

There was a rumble down the stairs and the boy poked his head in.

"Can you grab Mr. Constantine's clothes? They're next to my mending basket. There's a good lad."

Jack disappeared into the side room for a few moments before returning with the bundle of clothes, all folded. Martha took them from him.

"I noticed a bit of a tear in the shoulder there. I hope you don't mind that I mended it." She handed the pile over to him.

Byron's eyes widened. "You didn't need to do that, but thank you!"

"Oh, I needed a project anyhow. You can change in that room there, and I'll slice up some bread for you to take back to London."

"We wouldn't want to intrude on your hospitality more than we already have, Mrs. Davies," Fred said.

"It isn't a bother at all! We won't be able to eat all this bread on our own before it gets stale."

Byron allowed himself to be ushered into the other room. Once the door had closed behind him, he examined the stitches on the shoulder. The stitches were evenly placed and hidden neatly in the weave of the cloth. The tears caused by his encounter with the parrot were practically invisible. He chuckled to himself. Between Martha's hospitality, Harold's quick thinking, and Jack's quiet mischievousness, the Davies really were something else.

After getting dressed, Byron pulled his wallet from his

baggage and extracted a five-pound note, setting it on the side table to be found later. He opened the door just as Martha handed Fred a handkerchief of sliced bread. Jack was listening with wide eyes as Fred told the tales of their exploits.

"You mean my dad panicked the sheep on purpose?" Jack said, laughing.

"It was the only way to stop the barge!" Fred slapped his knee. "You should have seen them all, swimming along." He leaned towards Mrs. Davies. "They're fine, if you were wondering. Not a one of them was injured."

"I'm glad they had a bit of excitement before they got to Bristol," she said. "And that they helped you catch those thieves."

"They were integral to us catching them, actually." Byron straightened his collar as he stepped back into the main room. "As were all of you. We can't thank you enough."

"It was no trouble at all! I'm glad we could help," Mrs. Davies said.

Fred opened the door and Byron followed him out.

He paused by the bush. "There is one other thing, Mrs. Davies."

"Yes?" She pulled her shawl tighter around her shoulders.

"What sort of a bush is this?"

She stepped outside and smiled. "Oh, those are camellias. Lovely things, aren't they?"

Byron nodded. They were lovely. But why?

November 13, 1888

THEY STAYED ONE MORE NIGHT IN BERKSHIRE and Byron tossed and turned all night long. Somehow, he wasn't even concerned about what Commissioner Parry would say about their "failure" to solve the sheep panic, even though he ought to be. Instead, his mind kept drifting to those pink and white flowers. What was so important about camellias? What had he forgotten?

He'd managed to solve the case without his journal and even with minimal help from Fred. But without his journal there was no way for him to recall why camellias were so crucial. Was it for a previous case? Was it even important at all?

The sun crept through the windows and he sighed, getting up out of his thoughts rather than stew. Fred stirred, yawning and rubbing at his eyes, just after Byron had finished dressing.

"So, are you still set on citing lightning as the cause of ovine panic?" Fred said as he got ready for the day.

"Think of it this way," Byron said, happy to take his mind off of his forgetfulness for a moment. "If those boys hadn't caused a panic, the barge wouldn't have been delayed, and the thieves wouldn't have been caught. Why should we punish them for aiding us in a different investigation?"

"You make a good point. They definitely didn't understand the ramifications for spooking the flocks. And surely once we show Parry the solved case of burglary, all thoughts of sheep will be forgotten!" Fred laughed but sobered when he turned and saw Byron's expression.

"You alright there?" he asked.

"I've forgotten something," Byron said, not bothering to hide his unease. "I'm not sure what, but as soon as we're done speaking with the interim commissioner, I must find my journal."

"Sounds about right. Best get back to London then, eh?"

The train ride was too slow, as was the hansom cab that took them to Scotland Yard. Byron's head was filled with panicked thoughts. Each moment stretched into the next, anxiety increasing the longer he couldn't remember. Was this what the last four years had been like? This torture? It was as if he was living in a dream he couldn't escape from.

Fred sensed his mood and stayed quiet for the most part. Or perhaps he was tired from the ordeal as well. At any rate, they reached the interim commissioner's office just after one. His secretary smiled as they approached.

"May I help you?" A plaque on her desk said Lorelei Tawnsing. She had curly brown hair and green eyes, and for some reason that bothered Byron. Green eyes. That was important too, but he couldn't fathom why.

Fred spoke up as Byron's thoughts spiraled. "We're here to speak with Commissioner Parry. Is he in?"

"He is. I believe he should be able to see you, but let me check." She stood and knocked on the door, poking her head in a moment after. She turned to them. "Go on in."

Commissioner Parry sat at his desk, just as cantankerous as he had been the first time Byron had met with him in his office. He frowned as they came in. "You're back a day early. Have you solved the case?"

"We've solved two cases, actually." Byron moved forward. "We have a note from Colonel Blandy explaining the whole situation." He passed the note over.

Commissioner Parry raised an eyebrow at him but took the note, reading over the contents. His brow knitted together by the time he reached the end. "Art thieves? In Berkshire?"

"Not anymore," Fred said.

"And you say the sheep were startled by some lightning?"

"We interviewed several farmers in the area," Byron said. "All of them told the same story."

"That didn't take much detective work, did it?"

"Not especially, no. However, discovering and catching the thieves did," Byron said. "And you may want to reach out to the French police about a potential art collector dealing in stolen English paintings. Under the name Vermielle."

"Selene Vermielle?" Parry asked.

"That would be the one, sir," Fred bounced on his tiptoes.

"The same Vermielle that you released after"—Parry consulted a paper on his desk— "she gave some information involving Circe and the death of Mr. Pennington?"

Ah. That did explain why the name sounded familiar. Blast his memory!

Byron nodded. "I had the permission of Chief Inspector Thatcher, and considering that we managed to apprehend the killer because of Vermielle's efforts, I still stand by that decision."

"Hm." Parry leaned back.

"He's proved himself," Fred said. "Not that he needed to in the first place."

"Yes. I can see that." Parry picked up the letter from Blandy and glanced over it again. "I suppose I'll need to arrange for those men to go after Durant then, as per our agreement."

Byron frowned. He knew the name Durant. Alexander Durant. What had he done?

"And since you're so keen on catching him, I'll place your name on the roster to go after him."

Something about that seemed off. There was a reason for him to stay in London, wasn't there?

"Is there anything else?" Parry set the letter aside and clasped his hands on the desk.

"No, thank you, sir," Byron said as he and Fred turned to leave the room.

Once the door had closed behind them, Byron let out a sigh of relief.

Fred clapped him on the shoulder. "You've done it!"

"Correction, we've done it." Byron smiled. "I couldn't have done it without you."

"Oh, I'm sure you would have been fine. After all, you managed without your journal, well enough. Although, I am surprised you agreed to go to France."

"Well, we need to catch Durant, don't we?"

Fred laughed. "You're not dragging me into this one again."

Byron's smile faltered. The gaps in his memory were becoming more and more disconcerting.

Fred noticed the change in attitude and pulled him into an alcove. "Is something the matter?"

Byron shook his head. "There's something important, Fred. Something I'm missing. It's just out of reach."

Fred let out a slow breath. "Right, you mentioned that earlier. Do you know what it's about?"

"Not at all. It's all fuzzy. Like there's something blank where the memories are supposed to be."

"It'll come to you. And if not, your journal is sure to have it."

"Right. Right."

Fred led the way down the hall and towards the stairs. As they approached, Chief Inspector Thatcher came from the other side.

"Constantine! Wensley! It's good to see the two of you around again."

"You as well, Inspector," Fred said.

"I'd stay and chat, but it seems there's been an incident involving some swans in Kensington Gardens, and I've got to get down there."

"Swans?" Byron asked.

"Yes. Seems quite ridiculous, doesn't it? I'll see the two of you later." Thatcher hurried down the stairs.

"Swans." Byron frowned.

"Better than sheep, eh?" Fred joked.

Byron shook his head. "Swan Walk. *Mira.*" His breath quickened. He'd forgotten Mira! Shock and revulsion flooded through him. How could he have done that?

"Fred, I've got to go. Mira's been waiting almost a week for me and—" He rushed down the stairs.

"What about that thing you've forgotten?" Fred called after him.

"I've remembered!" Byron grinned as he ran out of Scotland Yard and onto the street.

He called for a hansom cab to get him there faster. How stupid could he be, forgetting the most important person in his life? It had been hardly a week, and yet here he was forgetting her all over again. On the other hand, he had remembered her on his own. That had to count for something, didn't it? How could he apologize?

A few blocks away from Swan Walk, he caught sight of a flower shop.

"Stop!" he told the driver, hopping down before the wheels had slowed. "I will just be a moment, can you wait?"

"I'll stay unless another customer comes by," the driver said.

A small bell rang as Byron entered the shop and the man behind the counter turned to greet him.

"May I help you, sir?"

"Yes. Do you have any camellias?"

The man blinked. "Yes, sir. They just came in this morning." He moved to the back room and returned with a vase filled to the brim with pink, white, and red camellias.

Byron tempered his smile. "Ah. Those are beautiful specimens."

"Aren't they? Did you have a preference as to what colours you wanted in your bouquet?"

The detective fingered the stem of the closest white camellia. Adoration didn't quite say enough, did it? His gaze drifted to the red. Would she perceive that as love or passion? Would that be too much? And what of the pink? Yes, he longed for her but how would she take any of this? Perhaps flowers were a silly idea.

He swallowed. "Do you have any suggestions?"

"You were the one who wanted camellias, sir."

"Well, yes. But." Byron cleared his throat. "That was because she mentioned it was her favorite flower. I didn't stop to think about what the colours meant."

The shopkeeper seemed to be aware of the turmoil in his very soul and nodded sagely. "Well, what do you want to say?"

"I want her to know that I love her. That I missed her. That I never want to forget her."

"I believe I can come up with something for you, sir."

The man went to work, picking different flowers and leaves from around the shop. Soon enough Byron had a bouquet of red and pink camellias, purple salvia and gladiolus, and white chrysanthemums. Flowers in hand and money out of it, Byron rushed out of the shop. Unfortunately, the hansom cab was nowhere to be found. But that didn't deter him a moment. Instead, he turned his steps down the road. Faster to go on foot rather than call down another cab.

The closer he came to Swan Walk, the more anxious he became. What would she think when she found out? Would she be hurt? Of course, she would. She had been before, even if she tried to hide it. Was there a way to soften the blow? Would the flowers be enough to beg her forgiveness?

And then there was the issue of avoiding this circumstance in the future. After all, he was going to France. He'd known there was a reason he didn't want to go. Why couldn't he have remembered her then? Now he'd have to leave her again. On the other hand, if he went after Durant himself, he could ensure that he was brought to justice and wouldn't be able to harm Mira again.

But was his proximity to Mira important to his remembering her? Or did he simply need to keep his journal on his person regardless of whether he needed it?

A strange feeling came over him. He'd forgotten her once, or more like hundreds of times before. What if he forgot her before he reached her residence? Had that ever happened before? There was no way of knowing. Which meant he needed to get there as soon as possible and see her for himself.

By the time he came to the house number in question he had worked himself into a sweat, and not with exercise. He gave a brisk knock on the door and willed his anxiety to calm down.

The butler opened it within a minute and panic gripped Byron as he wracked his brain for the name.

"Mr. Constantine." The butler stepped aside to let him pass. "May I take your things?"

"Yes, thank you, L . . .Landon?" Byron stuttered on the name, and his shoulders slumped in relief when the man said nothing to correct him. A quick catalogue of the other coats and hats on the hooks showed that the entire family would be at home. Landon added Byron's hat and coat to the rest and eyed the flowers in his hand.

"I'll bring a vase for those to the sitting room, if you'd care to find the way yourself. I'm sure Miss Blayse will be pleased to receive them."

"Thank you."

Byron took measured breaths as he moved towards the sitting room. Or at least, what he believed was the direction of the sitting room. For whatever reason, the furnishings around him prompted a sense of déjà vu, but didn't give any indication as to where he should go. He clenched his free hand. It shouldn't be a vague recollection! He'd been in the sitting room before, hadn't he? This should be simple. It was a house, not a labyrinth!

A familiar laugh rang out from behind him. He froze and turned towards the sound. It came from a room near the front of the house. That was Mira's laugh, wasn't it? The door was ajar and he took a moment to steel himself before pushing it open.

At first, he only saw her brother, whose name, once again, escaped him. Winston? Wesley? Whatever the name was, he was halfway through a move in a game of draughts. His gaze drifted to the seat opposite and he caught sight of her reddish-brown curls. His pulse quickened. There she was. Real. Right in front of him. He let out a silent breath of relief. What now? Mira's back was to the door, her foot propped up on the sofa, her ankle still healing. Neither she nor her brother noticed him as he stood in the doorway.

"Are you sure you want to make that move?" she said, and Byron's breath stilled at its euphonious timbre.

"I believe it's the only move I could make, given the circumstances." Her brother sat back, arms folded across his chest.

Mira leaned over the table, picked up one of her red pieces and delicately hopped it over three black pieces, successfully moving it to the other side of the board. Her curls bounced around her face as she laughed and said, "Crown me, my good Walker!"

Walker. The brother's name was Walker. How had he forgotten?

"How did I not see that?" Walker groaned and flipped her piece over.

"Perhaps you just aren't as observant as you thought," she teased.

"Oh really?" Walker smirked. "Well then, shall we invite Mr. Constantine to come in?"

Byron stiffened at his name as Mira's head whipped towards the door.

"Byron!" She faltered. Her eyes shone in the light streaming through the window and a pinkish rouge rose to her cheeks. "What are you doing here?"

His mouth hung open a moment or two as he thought over the question. There was something crucial that needed to be said, but now that she was in front of him, the purpose of his visit completely slipped his mind. As their expressions dipped closer towards confusion, he realized he was taking much too long to find his words.

"Er. Well. I just finished things up at Scotland Yard and well . . ." He took a step forward into the room, pausing to hide the bouquet behind his back. If she was questioning his presence, perhaps he shouldn't have come. "Should I not be here?"

Mira's cheeks reddened further and she shook her head,

fussing a bit with her clothing. "Not at all. I mean," she stuttered. "I just didn't expect you is all."

His muscles relaxed by a fraction.

Walker cleared his throat. "When did you get back?"

"Just this morning. How are the two of you?"

Mira blew some hair out of her face. "Positively bored. Walker keeps letting me win."

"That is not true." Walker stood and stretched. "I'm going to go see where Landon's popped off to. Maybe he can get us some sandwiches or tea or something. Do you want anything in particular, Constantine?"

Byron ripped his gaze from Mira's and shook his head. "No. Anything is fine."

Walker nodded and gave him a small smile as he left the room. The door clicked closed, and a heavy silence settled over the two of them. After a moment Mira leaned forward to put the draughts away.

"Did things work out with the Interim Commissioner?" she asked.

"Most definitely." Byron took a cautious step forward. He needed to tell her that he'd forgotten again. And that he was heading for France. But there was no way of telling her without hurting her. Which should come first? The flowers or the apology?

She glanced up at him and furrowed her brow. "Then why do I get the feeling that something is the matter?"

Byron shook his head. "Nothing's the matter. It's just been a long week."

"Well, come in then." Mira smiled at him, and it was like the sun bursting through clouds. She gestured to the seat across from her. "I want to hear all about it."

He took a short step forward, decision made. "I'll tell you everything I remember, but first." He pulled the bouquet out from behind his back. She gave a small gasp, eyes sparkling with delighted surprise. Her gaze darted back and forth between the flowers and him.

"Flowers? Why?" She laughed.

This is when he should apologize. Tell her that his memory had faltered again. Watch as that surprise and joy faded into hurt. But she was so happy, and frankly so was he. So instead, he gave her a soft smile and moved over to her, cupping her face with his hand. "I brought you spring."

About the Author

Natalie Brianne's love of writing might be traced back to an old Rainbow Macintosh Laptop she received for her 8th birthday. Perhaps it came from years of improv storytelling and the discipline of wonder. Or maybe, she was born to write and didn't realize it until her first book sprung out of her fingertips somewhere between a house in Pleasant Grove, Utah and a bus on its way to Edinburgh, Scotland.

She received her degree in Interdisciplinary Humanities from BYU. While she could have studied English or Creative Writing, she opted to learn more about culture, distant lands, and people in hopes of writing better stories. Much of her first book, Constantine Capers: The Pennington Perplexity was written when she lived at 27 Palace Court, London, walking the streets as if she were her characters.

When Natalie isn't writing, voice acting, playing the guitar very badly, traveling, and forgetting that she has vegetables in her fridge.

CONSTANTINE CAPERS SERIES:

The Pennington Perplexity
Flashes of Memory
There Comes a Midnight Hour

THE 13TH ZODIAC SAGA:

Keepers of the Zodiac
Heart of the Meridian

SHORT STORIES AND NOVELLAS:

FROM CONSTANTINE'S CASEBOOK

Byron's Oblivion
The Great Sheep Panic
In the SIlence of the Catacombs

FROM SAMIRA'S SKETCHBOOK

A Constantine Christmas

GENERAL FICTION

The Glade of Sionn O' Shea